CYCLONE

Julia van Gorder

CYCLONE

Julia van Gorder

COTEAU BOOKS

Excerpt from "Ypres: 1915" from *Bread and Wine and Salt*, by Alden Nowlan, reproduced by permission from Stoddart Publishing Co. Limited, Canada.

Edited by Geoffrey Ursell
Cover and book design by Duncan Campbell.
Cover painting by Richard Widdifield.

Coteau Books acknowledges the financial support of: the Government of Canada through the Canada Council for the Arts and the Department of Canadian Heritage Book Publishing Industry Development Program; the Government of Saskatchewan through the Saskatchewan Arts Board; and the City of Regina through the Regina Arts Commission, for our publishing activities.

Coteau Books celebrates the 50ᵗᴴ Anniversary of the Saskatchewan Arts Board, and the 40ᵗᴴ Anniversary of the Canada Council for the Arts with this publication.

Canadian Cataloguing in Publication Data

Van Gorder, Julia, 1923—
Cyclone
ISBN 1-55050-127-5

I. Title.

PS8593.4543   C9 1998   C813'.54   C98-920015-9

Coteau Books
401-2206 Dewdney Avenue
Regina, Saskatchewan
Canada   S4R 1H3

AVAILABLE IN THE U.S. FROM:

General Distribution Services
85 River Rock Road, Suite 202
Buffalo, New York
USA   14207

*for Frances Jackson Ayre
who loves and remembers*

What's the word for a cyclone
when its movement is over?

—PABLO NERUDA

it makes me feel good knowing
that in some obscure, conclusive way
they were connected with me
and me with them

—ALDEN NOWLAN "YPRES: 1915"

CHAPTER 1

June 30, 1912, Regina, Saskatchewan

That hot, sticky afternoon Agnes Jackson sat on the back stoop plucking and cleaning the seven wild prairie chickens her son Arnold had shot that morning. She knew that her family would not eat all seven for supper that evening, and that Deborah would be the one to howl and spit out the shot pellets Agnes missed. Edward and Arnold would get a chicken each; she and the three girls would get half one each. She wondered if the remaining three birds would keep in the ice box if she roasted them with the others.

Agnes had left her corset off when she changed from her church clothes to a house dress. No one would see. No one came. She went into the vegetable garden and picked some string beans for supper. The clay soil was cracked, there being no water to spare for the garden. Edward's hens hunched in their coop. His two white geese with the chicory flower eyes, who usually ran at her for handouts, were hiding in the raspberries against the back fence. No wonder. Arnold had warned her by letter of the cold, but not of this insufferable heat.

Agnes moved into the kitchen and stuffed the birds with moistened bread crumbs, onions, suet, lemon juice, parsley, salt and pepper. Jessie would peel the potatoes when the girls came back from their stroll to Victoria Park to see the Dominion Day decorations. She left the beans in the sink – perhaps Miriam would cut them for her. She didn't like to ask too much of Deborah and Miriam now that they had jobs and contributed money to the family. In the ice box she had a trifle made from raspberries, gelatine, and last week's pound cake. Later she would make some Bird's Custard to cover it.

Agnes riddled the grate of her new McClary cookstove and added two lumps of coal. She glanced at the clock in the dining room. Now for her weekly bath, her time to herself. Going upstairs she saw her husband, Edward, sitting in his Sunday suit on the front porch, reading the latest *Manchester Guardians*, come in the post from The Old Country. Agnes began to churn. Do not bring Father, Arnold had written her. Why had she done it?

After she drew a cool tub, grateful for the miracle of indoor plumbing, she put Epsom salts in the water to soften it. She undressed, climbed into the tub, and lay back. Her hour to herself. The words of a poem surfaced. Whose was it? She filled the sponge with water and trickled it over her body as she chanted:

I live for those who love me
whose hearts are kind and true
for the heaven that smiles above me
and awaits my spirit too
For all human ties that bind me
for the task by God assigned me
for the bright hopes left behind me
and the good that I can do

At the phrase "bright hopes left behind me," her eyes filled and she was a girl back in Manchester, driving to the opera with her brother Lennie in the carriage and pair her father had given her for her birthday. Then Arnold's letter intruded in her reverie, "<u>Do not bring Father.</u>" She had written Arnold in 1910 that she *had* to follow him to Canada – there was no money for food and rent in Manchester. She had kept to herself – she hoped Arnold and the girls did not guess it – that Edward was a gambler. He kept trying to make money without working for it. Arnold had been silent when he saw his father get off the train in Regina with the rest of the family. Agnes had said to his back, "What could I do? We are a family, and we look after each other."

Edward had already retreated into his own world of silence. Arnold copied him. He did what he had to do to find shelter and food for the family, first on Osler Street, and now he had built this house because there were none to rent. But he kept to himself. And silence hung over the family when Arnold or Edward were in the room. Agnes had given up trying to penetrate their silences.

In her mind Agnes began to reason with her son. Although Edward had not found himself a job in Regina, he did the gardening and raised and cared for the chickens and the two white geese in the back yard. Arnold enjoyed for his breakfast the eggs his father had produced. And Edward had grown wonderful vegetables that supplied their table. And he did do repairs around the house. Not that much was needed in this new house.

Agnes dipped her head back in the water and washed her thin gray hair with coal tar soap. She rinsed it under the tap. Then she scrubbed herself with Lifebuoy soap, rinsed it off, towelled herself and sprinkled *4711 eau de cologne* under her arms and *Ashes-of-roses* talcum powder under her pendulous breasts. She twisted her hair into a bun and washed her underclothes in the tub water with the bar of Fels Naptha laundry soap she kept in the bathroom. Then she checked the covered bucket in the lavatory to see if either of the older girls had left menstrual rags soaking. Yes, there were three of them. Agnes threw them in the tub. She wondered if the girls had prepared Jessie for her monthly periods. She found it so difficult to discuss bodily matters with her children.

She dressed in her second-best moiré dress and went downstairs to hang the washing outside with towels laid over it so that the neighbours would not see the family's private life, particularly on a Sunday. Things would dry in no time in this heat.

No sooner had she got the washing hung out than she was chilled. The leaden air turned yellow. Flashes of lightning and angry thunder. Big splashes of rain. Agnes fought against a sudden wind to bring the washing in, then rushed around the house closing windows. Some blinds had rolled up. When she went to shut the front door, Edward was still reading newspapers on the front porch.

Rain and hail pelted down.

"The farmers will lose their crops," Agnes called.

Edward looked at her as if to say, "So?"

Agnes hated his superiority, his distance from life. "That will affect us all."

The wind roared. "The girls!" Agnes realized. "Edward, put on your coat, take an umbrella, and find them. They're over at Victoria Park in their muslin dresses and parasols."

Edward turned a page of his paper. No use, no use at all.

Agnes went into the hall, wrapped a shawl around her shoulders, took Edward's umbrella, and walked into the deluge. At Rae Street a cross wind blew the umbrella inside out. Then it blew out of sight. Further down Twelfth Avenue, shingles and glass and bricks were flying, windows were making a popping noise as the wind sucked them out.

She walked into devastation, her skirt and petticoat, soaking wet, clung from her knees to her ankles. People were groaning for help or walking dazed, as she was. Agnes pushed on – her girls, her innocent girls. The public buildings, the churches in Victoria Square, all were wrecked. Masonry and boards cluttered the sidewalks. Pulling at her wet skirts, Agnes stepped over them, around them, as in a nightmare, calling to her girls. They were not there.

The storm blew over as suddenly as it had hit. The Power House siren wailed. Rescue crews formed. Squads of Mounties arrived to organize the helpers. Outside the YMCA a young man in his Sunday suit cradled a fair young man, unconscious, a nasty gash bleeding down his face. The injured man wore only trousers and suspenders over a singlet.

A mounted policeman leaned down from his horse. "Any broken bones, sir?"

The injured young man opened his green eyes, stared, then closed them.

"None that I could feel," his friend answered.

Agnes knocked on the Mountie's boot. "Girls! Three girls in white dresses. With parasols."

The Mountie looked around Victoria Square. He shook his head, then leaned to Agnes. "Madam? Is your house intact?"

"Yes. Yes it is."

"Where is it?"

"2929 Twelfth Avenue."

"Then between you, would you kindly get this injured

man to your house, and we'll send a doctor if you're worried."

Agnes looked at the young man in the Sunday suit. Together they bent to lift the injured man.

CHAPTER 2

June 30, 1912

The Jackson girls had not gone to Victoria Park to see the Dominion Day decorations. When they reached Rae Street, where their father could not see them, Miriam took both sisters by the the arm and ran them across 12th Avenue. "Come on! We're going to Wascana Lake. It will be cool there."

"Stop it!" Deborah said. "Mother expects us to do as we say."

"She would never agree to our going to the lake. Come on. Arnold will be there with his friend Jack, and perhaps they'll take us on the lake in a boat."

"But Mother says..."

"Mother says, Mother says. When are you going to grow up? You're seventeen and earning your own money. Make up your own mind."

Jessie, the youngest, was captive to the thought of a boat ride. With Miriam, she pulled Deborah along, their high boots clacking on the wooden sidewalks.

Arnold and Jack Foxxe were carrying Jack's canoe on their shoulders when the girls hailed them. Arnold was not pleased to see his sisters. He wondered if his mother had sent them, trying to trap him into looking after them. He turned his back on them. He and Jack put the boat in the water.

Jack Foxxe was pleased. He had grown up an only child. He envied Arnold the life that three sisters must bring. He already admired Miriam, the dark beauty, but the canoe would hold only three.

"Look, Buster, why don't we take turns taking the girls out?"

The girls doubled with laughter to hear Arnold called Buster. From that day that's what they called him.

Who would stay behind? As they argued, the temperature dropped, there were flashes of fork lightning on the southern horizon, rolls of thunder. Strong winds raced across the lake, chilling the girls who hugged each other. The air turned eerie green, the water dull yellow. Jessie pointed to dark storm clouds in the south-west. "Look, that cloud has a tail!"

Arnold, smelling ozone, pointed to black clouds also forming a funnel beside the new legislative building in the south-east.

"Run for your lives," Jack shouted at the girls. "Buster and I will save the canoe." Jack had experienced tornados in his travels with his parents.

Led by Deborah, the girls started towards Lorne Street.

"No, not that way. Up Albert Street." Jack called.

The girls ran towards Albert Street, afraid only of getting wet. Then they cut over to Rae Street and finally Retallack.

Arnold and Jack were lifting the canoe out of the water when the wind, roaring, wrenched it out of their hands. They were knocked flat, their straw boaters whisking off.

"Hang onto a tree," Jack called. But the saplings, newly planted, blew away, scraping Arnold's hands. The two men sprawled on the ground. They clung to the holes the trees had left, their jackets flapping over their heads. Tons of howling water swirled over them, on them.

Arnold felt a warm flood of fear down his trousers. "Oh, God, save me."

The storm blew over as quickly as it had come.

"Right. Let's follow the path of the storm and find my canoe," Jack said, scrambling to his feet as if not much had happened. He was caked in mud and his light jacket was ripped up the back. He held part of a sapling in one hand.

Arnold got up cautiously. He felt his face and hair. Mud. He tried to straighten and dust his jacket and trousers, but they too were caked in gumbo. His trousers might dry without Jack noticing. He would go home when they reached Twelfth Avenue, saying he had to check on his family.

They headed up Lorne Street into destruction. Cars had been turned over like barrels. Houses had collapsed into rubble. Some owners were on the street looking lost, some hurt. Arnold wanted to stop and help, but what could he do? He gave his clean handkerchief to a man who was cradling his injured wife. "I'll send an ambulance," he said.

Sloshing through water inches deep, Arnold caught up with Jack. He was studying a horse lying groaning in the road. It was harnessed to an overturned cart. The young men tried to free the horse, but they could not lift it to undo the harness on the underside.

"Should I go for my gun and shoot it?" Jack asked.

"I'm not sure the owners would be pleased," Arnold said grimly.

"Right. On to the canoe."

In Victoria Square where the havoc was greatest, a

mounted policeman asked them if they had a car to get the wounded to hospital. Jack went off to get his parents' car. Arnold was assigned to look for casualties under the rubble of the Telephone Exchange, the interior of which had collapsed. Some of the telephone girls, who had been working at the switchboard, were missing.

Jack's canoe was later found in the north end of the city, on Lorne Street. It had been blown through the window of a house.

When the Jackson girls got back to Twelfth Avenue they saw their mother, her clothes clinging to her ample figure, helping a wet young man drag a wounded man up the steps of the house. Father was nowhere to be seen. The girls ran to help. Agnes gave them an exasperated look. They lifted the wounded man onto the green tapestry chesterfield and covered him with an afghan. Deborah ran for a face cloth. When Charles Wilson opened his eyes, it was Deborah he saw and felt, dabbing his wound.

"Now, you lot, get out of those wet things. And Jessie, show this young man the bathroom and give him a clean towel from the linen cupboard. Miriam, go to Arnold's room and find him some dry clothing." Agnes then called after them, "And bring some dry clothes down for this poor man."

The kettle was always on the boil. Agnes made tea while Deborah buttered Welsh cakes, and Miriam cut pound cake. Agnes told Jessie to take tea upstairs to her father. She assumed Edward had retired to the bedroom rather than deal with the crisis.

The short young man in Arnold's clothing towelled his friend, then put him in a pair of Arnold's striped flannelette pjamas. The invalid kept waking and trying to get up, but would doze off.

When he was seated at the dining table, the helpful young man smiled at Jessie when she passed him Welsh cakes. He lifted one up. "The first I have seen since I left home."

Agnes listened to his voice. The young were quick to dampen the cadence of their British accents to the flat long vowels of Canadians. "So you're a Welshman, are you?"

"Born and bred. But my mother was Belgian. I spoke three languages at home. My father teaches school. Charles..." he nodded at the invalid, "was born in Ontario. My name is Louis Rhys."

"We're the Jacksons from Manchester. We came last year. When did you come over?"

"In February. I've been sharing a room at the YMCA with Charles – rooms are that hard to find here – and the roof of the building just flew off," he raised his short arms and small hands, "and the floor collapsed on Charles's side. I clung to an upright and slid down it. My hands are full of slivers."

"Jessie, get a needle from my workbox, and start to work."

Jessie, an awkward child of twelve, bent over Louis Rhys's hands.

"Oh, you're all thumbs. Deborah, you'd best do it."

The seven prairie chickens came in handy for supper. Edward came down for his meal and was introduced to Louis and Charles. He was gruff, then silent. Agnes heated "pobs" for Charles – bread soaked in warm milk.

Arnold did not appear. At first Agnes did not fret. He

was often tardy, but he always phoned if he were not coming. She went to the telephone. The line was dead.

The handsome young Mountie, Tom Richards, came to check on Charles. Agnes gave him food, which he insisted on eating standing by the door. Miriam noticed that he wore a wedding band. Deborah and Jessie ran outside to give his horse sugar cubes and a carrot.

Before he left, Tom Richards looked at Louis Rhys, comfortable in one of Arnold's pullovers. Louis was puzzled, then he jumped up. "You need help down there, don't you?"

"It's all right. Finish your tea, but there's lots to be done."

Charles tried to stand. Tom Richards walked over and put his hands on Charles's shoulders. "It's all right, chum. You'd better stay quiet for a day or two."

As the men left Agnes said, "Louis, there will be a bed made up for you here whenever you get back." She could feel Edward stiffen behind her. She felt a surge of energy. She was needed, and this was her home, her son had built it for her.

"Now, you lot," she said to the girls. "Miriam, make a bed for Jessie on that box in our room. Use a quilt for a mattress. Deborah, you and Miriam move into the double bed in Jessie's room. Change the beds in your room for Charles here and Louis when he gets back." She turned to Charles. "We'll have you snug in bed in no time."

Edward went out to the garden to feed and settle the fowl.

Deborah took her mother aside. "Mam, there're aren't enough sheets," she said. Agnes thought. Then she took Deborah by the elbow into the box room under the stairs. They lifted cartons aside until they reached a handsome wooden box. "Run up to my dresser set and fetch the little key in the covered box," she whispered. Deborah brought the key, which opened the chest. It was full of new folded white linens, all embroidered in white with the initials MS. Deborah picked one up and held it to her cheek. It was so much smoother than the flannelette sheets they used winter and summer. But they had never had house guests before. Deborah pointed to the initials. Her mother shook her head, as if this were their secret.

After the beds had been changed, Agnes wondered which of her daughters she could send out to look for Arnold, although God knows what part of the city he was in. He didn't tell her where he was going when he was out, or when he would be back. Miriam was the brightest, but she was so willful, she might tuck into the work that needed doing and forget her mother's worry about Arnold's safety. Deborah had less sense. She would start talking, asking questions, and also forget why she was there. Jessie was still biddable. And there was an hour of daylight left. She would send Jessie over to Victoria Square.

When she walked the seven short blocks to the square, Jessie could not believe the change in what had become familiar. Someone's piano was out on the sidewalk, its keyboard slanting up at an angle. When she went onto the road to get around the piano, her boots sank deep in mud. Three black and white cows were roaming the street. Jessie climbed on the wooden sidewalk again, hoping the cows would not notice her. She followed an old woman carrying a cat in one arm and a canary cage in the other. The old woman disappeared into the crowds in the square.

Firemen were hosing several buildings. Walking carefully around clutters of broken glass and wood, Jessie found Arnold working with other men on the wreckage that had been the Central Telephone Office. She stood beside Arnold waiting for him to notice her. He was covered in mud. His partner lifting at this site was Louis. Arnold smiled at Jessie. "This clean man's wearing my clothes," he chided.

"Yes, he and Mam brought an injured man home," she said.

"Well, tell your mother I'm all right, and I'll be home when the work is done."

He turned back to the shifting of debris. Then he turned to her again. "Tell her we've found no bodies." Louis seemed to snap awake at that realization. He looked at Jessie but seemed not to recognize her.

Arnold was transferred to clear the rubble outside the YMCA. He had not felt so vigorous since building 2929 12th Avenue. The storm had blown over, leaving the air cooly pleasant. His job at the hardware store was not physically demanding. Here he was given a London street boy, Billy, as a partner. His accent was so thick that none of the other men could understand him. Arnold lapsed into his school dialect when talking to him. Billy liked to act as foreman, to decide to which heap they would transfer bricks, boards, furniture and personal possessions. He liked to call "Heave, heave" when there were heavy beams to lift. He wants to be useful, Arnold guessed.

When dusk came and lanterns were lit, a short round figure with heavy feet came round the corner from Twelfth Avenue. It was Agnes, with a honey tin of tea and a basket of sandwiches and jam tarts. She looked at Arnold, gave a sigh of relief, then served food. Arnold was proud of his mother. She was the first to come, to realize the workers would be hungry.

He used to love her when he was young. Why had that changed? Now he loved only Miriam.

CHAPTER 3

January 2, 1900, Withington, Manchester, England

Ademanding knock on the door.

"Don't answer that," Agnes said. She was sitting in the rocking chair in the kitchen, nursing the new baby.

Miriam could see the large shape of Mrs. Bowich through the coloured glass of the front door. "Tell Mother it's Mrs.Bowich," she whispered to Deborah.

Deborah ran to Mother. "It's Mrs. Bowich."

Agnes looked with despair at her untidy kitchen. Again the knocking. "Oh, let her in."

Mrs. Bowich came in her apron, the sleeves of her cotton frock rolled past the elbow. She was carrying a tray of treacle buns which she set on the wooden table top along with a bottle of Guiness. "I wondered if you'd delivered, Mrs. Jackson. You looked so peaked on Sunday in the yard. Then when we got this note this morning, I knew." She chuckled, giving the note to Agnes, and pulling the blanket away from the baby. "I hear it's another girl. You could have done with a boy to balance things."

Agnes's face flamed when she read the note. *We have a*

kid we do not want. Her jaw set. She put the note in her pocket.

"That would be your Arnold," Mrs. Bowich said of the note. She lifted the baby. "But I don't want to keep this one, lovely lass that she is. We've enough mouths to feed in the Bowich family."

"Thank you for the buns," Agnes said. "You've been busy already this morning then."

"What are you going to call her?" Mrs. Bowich asked Deborah. Mrs. Bowitch lifted an iron from the range and began to iron Edward's shirts, which were airing on the overhead rack. Agnes wished she wouldn't. Even the turned collars and cuffs were fraying. But everyone was poor these days.

"We're going to call her Jessica," Miriam said. Although only five, she had become the spokesperson for Deborah, who was seven.

"Are we now, Miss?" Agnes said. "We'll see about that."

"You'd best drink that stout, Mrs. Jackson. Do you a world of good. You've got a lot on your plate."

"When have I not had a lot on my plate, Mrs. Bowich?" But Agnes did not drink the stout. She saved it in the cold pantry for Edward, who was also depressed at another mouth to feed.

When Edward came home from the shop, he poured himself the stout, then sat in the rocking chair to read *The Guardian*. Agnes was at the range, heating shepherd's pie for tea. She took the note out of her pocket and handed it to him. "This is what your son has been up to," she said. "The neighbours."

When Arnold came home from school, proud of his success as a scholar, Edward stood up and whacked him across the head, scattering his books and school cap across the slate floor. Agnes had been scrubbing that floor when her labour pains started. "That will teach you to tell the neighbours our business," Edward said.

"But you were the one to say that," Arnold said. "I was only quoting you." His cheeks, like Agnes's, flamed easily.

Edward struck him again. "Don't you go telling the neighbours what I say in my own house! Is there no privacy?"

Arnold wailed. Miriam picked up the books and cap.

"Outside with that caterwauling!" Edward said.

"No," said Agnes. "We don't want the neighbours to hear that." She felt blood flooding out of her onto the towelling clutched between her legs. She would have to go out to the lavatory and change it.

The baby was whimpering again.

"Then upstairs to bed with you without your tea," Edward said.

"I have to go to the lavatory," Arnold said to his mother, desperation in his voice.

"Then go and be quick about it," Agnes said, leaning against the kitchen table, hoping to staunch her flow. She knew Arnold would wet his trousers before he got out to the lavatory, and she would have to wash them and hide them from Edward.

When Edward went back to the shop to relieve his brother-in-law, Bob, Agnes sent Deborah and Miriam up to Arnold with two treacle buns and a cup of tea. Deborah spilled the tea on the stairs.

Arnold jumped out of bed and stood at the top of the staircase. "Oh, that Borah," he said. "She's two bricks short of a load."

Miriam took the buns to Arnold, wiped up the spill, and took Arnold another cup of tea. Agnes set Deborah to rocking the new baby.

In Arnold's room – he was the only one to have a room to himself – Miriam sat at the foot of his bed and watched her brother eat. His books lay scattered across his covers. She hoped he would recover enough to give her a reading lesson.

"I'm going to kill him when I grow up," Arnold told her, licking his fingers as he ate his treacle buns. Miriam went to get him a wet flannel to wipe the sticky off his hands.

"No," she said. "You can't do that."

"Why not? I can do anything when I'm a grown-up."

"Because the ten commandments tell us not to kill, and to honour our father and our mother. And the New Testament tells us to love those who spitefully use us."

"Where'd you hear that? At his church, or hers?"

"Both."

The children were taken to the Primitive Methodist Church in Mosside with their mother Sunday mornings, and to evensong at St. John's Anglican church with their father.

Miriam could hear the clatter of clogs of the men and women who worked in the mills. She moved to the window to watch them. They would be walking home from work. One woman was picking up the droppings from the dray horses delivering to the Red Lion, putting the droppings in a sack she carried. Did she use them for fuel or for the garden?

"Well, I can't see honouring them, whatever that means, without loving them. After all, they don't love or honour us," Arnold went on.

"How can you say that? I'm sure our mother loves us."

"I think she sees us as just another mouth to feed, another pair of hands to do the chores."

"Miriam?" Agnes called from downstairs. "You come down to the scullery and dry these tea things."

"I love you. You're the only one. You know that, don't you?"

Did she hear him? She was running down the stairs.

It was dusk when Agnes came to comfort her son. She was cradling the sleeping baby. She tried to rub Arnold's towsled head for comfort, but he pushed her hand away.

"Why did you tell him?" Arnold asked. "He wouldn't have hit me if you hadn't told him."

Agnes listened thoughtfully to the ivy the wind was scratching across the window. She didn't know why she had told him.

"The baby is one of us now," she said. "We're a family, and we must look after each other."

"But he said he didn't want it."

"Well, there isn't much money to feed six mouths. But we'll manage. We always do. When you're fourteen, you'll have to work. That'll make things easier."

"I'm going to be a teacher," Arnold said.

"Oh, you can put that idea out of your head right now. You're going to have to work for wages to help support your sisters."

"That's his job, isn't it? And why does he have the right to be cross, to be catered to?"

"He's losing his teeth. D'you know what that means to a man? And there's no money to buy false ones."

"Is that why he wears a beard?"

"No, I imagine he wears a beard because the king does. It's the thing to do. It's good for business."

"I will never grow a beard."

"You might, you might not. Who knows."

"I'm going to be an engineer like Uncle Lennie. I'll work for him."

Agnes couldn't tell her son again there was no money for him to go to Grammar School, let alone college. She thought of her brother Lennie, who was prosperous, married and living in Plymouth. She sat in silence at the foot of her son's bed, and fingered the quilt, which she had made from worn-out sheets.

"You're going to have to choose between him and me, Mother. You know that, don't you?"

Agnes said nothing. She hoped that would not happen. Life was made up of loyalties, the queen said. Again the ivy scratching the window. Was it a message?

"Sing to me," Arnold said, frustrated by his mother's retreats into silence. He never knew what she was really thinking.

Still cradling the baby, Agnes moved to the window and sang,

Sweet and low, sweet and low
Wind of the western sea
Low, low, breathe and blow
Wind of the western sea!

Over the rolling waters go
Come from the dying moon and blow
Blow him again to me
While my little one, while my pretty one sleeps

Sleep and rest, sleep and rest
Father will come to thee soon
Rest, rest, on Mother's breast

"No! Don't sing that verse. I hate it, I hate him."

Agnes, startled, stopped singing. She came back and sat on his bed, holding his large hand with her free one. But the song sang on inside her.

Father will come to thee soon
Father will come to his babe in the nest
Silver sails sailing out of the west
Send him again to me
While my little one, while my pretty one sleeps

Send him again to me...How often had she sung that as a girl when Martin was away at sea. And when he returned...when he returned that last time to marry her...overcome with passion and longing, he had made improper advances to her. She had known nothing. Why had her mother told her nothing – when she was engaged to be married? She had dismissed Martin, locking away in her hope chest all her linens with his initials embroidered on them. She married instead the handsome widower, Edward Jackson, so like the Prince of Wales in appearance. He had awakened her to passion and knowledge of life, as Martin would have done. Yes, Martin, now captain of his own small vessel, would have been a better provider. He was a worker. She could see the house he had bought up the hill when he married that Iris Smith. Did he buy there to be near her? Did he ever think of her?

"What are you thinking, Mother?" Arnold asked. "I never know what you are thinking in your silences."

"I was just musing," she said.

CHAPTER 4

July 2, 1912, Regina, Saskatchewan

Jessie was the one to get a proper education, Agnes had decided. The others had to work to put food on the table, but Jessie was going to graduate from high school for the family.

But things were not going well for Jessie at school. When the family had arrived from England last year, the other children had laughed at her and her funny clothes, which were hand-me-downs from her sisters. They called her "the English kid." There was so much she didn't know. She had to unlearn pounds, shillings, and pence and be able to answer in dollars and cents. And her mother wouldn't let her run after the ice wagon and suck on chips of ice that fell on the road the way other kids could.

Miriam, who was the sempstress of the family, remade some of Jessie's clothes, and provided money for Canadian shoes and a coat. But still Jessie looked a boney, ungainly girl. They doubted that she would find a husband.

Agnes had Jessie chant her times tables while she peeled potatoes in the kitchen. Then she could sit in the rocking chair to read the daily paper to Agnes, who was grinding the rump of the roast to make shepherd's pie.

> *The Leader, July 2, 1912 – All Hello Girls Okay.*
> *All the girls in the telephone exchange are safe.*
> *Miss Black, said to be dying, was not in the build-*
> *ing at all. Miss Russel, supposed to have suffered*
> *a broken back, is not as badly injured as reported*
> *and will live.*

Agnes seized the newspaper from Jessie, saying, "Stop that nonsense and give me the real news." She pointed to another column.

> *Twenty eight Reginans were killed, over 200 are*
> *injured, and 2500 are homeless in the wake of the*
> *tornado that hit our city Sunday afternoon. Five*
> *hundred buildings have been destroyed.*

Jessie looked at her mother, then stumbled on.

> *Two storms at the south end of Wascana lake*
> *joined to form a funnel behind the new copper*
> *dome of the Legislative Assembly. The vortex of the*
> *storm, travelling at an estimated five hundred*
> *miles an hour, slashed through the legislative*
> *grounds, across Wascana Lake, north along Lorne*
> *Street, tearing a two-block swath through the*
> *downtown section, decorated with flags and*
> *bunting for Dominion Day, and five blocks into*
> *the north side.*
> *No buildings in the tornado's direct path*
> *withstood the onslaught of the winds. Houses*
> *have been smashed to rubble, and major buildings*

bordering on Victoria Park – the Metropolitan Methodist Church, Knox Presbyterian Church, the Baptist Church, the YMCA, the YWCA, the new Carnegie Library, the Methodist parsonage are all damaged, and rescue workers are still digging in the rubble looking for survivors. The cupola of the Baptist Church was found 3 blocks away. The telephone Exchange building was completely destroyed, but ten employees escaped with minor injuries. In the Railroad yard box cars were tossed about, and warehouses scattered like paper. The 75,000 bushel grain elevator disappeared. In all, close to five hundred buildings have been destroyed. Lorne Street, Smith Street, and Railway Street North and South seem to have suffered the worst. The damaged area is so sharply defined that people living to the east and west of the catastrophe did not know.

The City has borrowed 250 tents from the NWMP, and has cots set up in schools for the homeless. The City has also organized clearance and rescue crews.

The citizens of Regina have rallied admirably, housing and feeding the homeless.

"Stop right there," Agnes said, wiping her eyes from chopping onions. "I had no idea it was so bad. Now off you go to Mr. Darke, the butcher, and see if he has two pounds of pork sausage meat left. Pork, mind. Not beef."

Agnes would make sausage rolls to take to the rescue crews. While she waited for Jessie, she made Welsh cakes on the griddle.

Agnes fed her table the usual Tuesday shepherd's pie and lemon pudding. Her men had come home for dinner, and announced that only the Methodist Church was left to clear. Then their work would be done, and the city crews would take over sorting the valuables, the salvageables. The volunteers had to dig only for humans.

It was dusk when dinner was cleaned up. Agnes wrapped a shawl around her shoulders and took a lantern, a basket of food, and a tin of tea to Victoria Square. The square was full of people with lanterns, gathered around the workers clearing the rubble at the Metropolitan Methodist, her church. She nodded to members of the congregation that she recognized, and she smiled at Louis, when he looked up from lifting boards and bricks. He was a member of this church too.

The men were working too hard to stop and eat her food, and she didn't want to pass it to the onlookers. At about ten o'clock a foreman spoke to the minister of the church. He cleared his throat and announced that, Praise God, no more bodies had been found. He nodded to the choirmaster, who lifted an arm and all the people in the square sang, *"Praise God from whom all blessings flow."* Agnes poured a cup of tea. It was passed among the workers. She followed with her basket of sausage rolls and Welsh cakes.

Louis Rhys took her arm and escorted her home down Twelfth Avenue. Agnes was glad she had immigrated. She liked Regina. She liked this young man. He was steady and he sang in the choir of her church. He had a regular job at The Glasgow House, Men's Wear Department. He would be a good match for Deborah. They were both singers – Deborah sang in the choir of St. Paul's Anglican – and neither was tall. Yes, he would be a good match.

CHAPTER 5

July 2, 1912

Arnold had twice brought Billy home for a bath, food, and a rest. While working he had noticed Billy, in sorting personal possessions, slip a watch into his pocket. Walking home down Twelfth Avenue Arnold said to Billy in dialect, "About that watch in your pocket. Not a good idea to keep it. Could cause trouble. Why don't you get a job and buy yourself one?"

Billy brought out the watch and gave it to Arnold. "It's awright t' tlk C'nadian t' me. Else oil niver learn. Oi ony put it in pocket fer safekeepin'."

"I know. But that might be misunderstood and you might get punished for being so careful. Better to give the valuables over to the police."

"Besides, jobs hard t'come by Canada."

"They are for all of us. But there will be jobs clearing this mess up. And if you're a hard honest worker, which you are, you will get a job."

Arnold had asked to be wakened after four hours, when he and Billy set out again, Billy in some of Arnold's clothes. They sent Louis home for his four-hour break.

After the Methodist church had been cleared by lamp-
light and the mayor declared the crisis over, Arnold
realized that Billy, a Barnardo's boy, had nowhere to go. He
had been sent to Saskatchewan to work for his board for a
poor farmer, who had little enough food and supplies for
his family. In summer Billy had slept in the barn. In winter
he was allowed to sleep on the kitchen floor. He had run
away to Regina looking for lighter work that paid. Arnold
knew what it was to be bullied, to work to exhaustion on
a farm. But at least he loved his Aunt Fannie and Uncle
George, and they had worked as hard as he had.

The military had provided a number of collapsible canvas cots in Victoria Square. Arnold and Billy carried one
home to 2929 with two donated army blankets.

"Billy is going to sleep in our basement until he finds
work," Arnold announced to Agnes, who met them on the
porch. Her sleeves were rolled up.

Edward still sat on the porch smoking a cigar, a newspaper on his lap, although the sun had long gone down.

Agnes looked at Billy's large eyes, chicory flower blue like
the geese, and wondered what poor woman had borne him,
given him those eyes, then abandoned him. His fleshy bottom
lip was split in the middle, showing a trace of blood. He
chewed the left side of his lip with green-rimmed gray teeth.
Agnes's upbringing in the Primitive Methodist Church surged.
"No," she said. "There are no second-class citizens sleeping in
basements in our house. You men clear the box room under
the stairs. Put the boxes and the trunk in the basement."

When they moved inside, Edward got up, reached inside
the door for his cane – he was not overweight or lame, but
King Edward VII had always walked with a cane. Edward
walked on the streets until it was dark.

When Arnold had been building 2929, when he realized

that he was going to own this house, he agreed with Jack's suggestion to put a second toilet in the basement. Arnold had already set a light and a mirror over the two cement laundry tubs down there. With three young women in the house, the pressure on one bathroom was too much when one had to get out to work. So Arnold already kept his shaving things in the basement next to his mother's blue-ing bags and laundry soap. He hung his towel and face cloth on the drying rack overhead. He invited the other young men to use this space, which they did.

Agnes scrubbed out the box room and found one extra of her good sheets, which she doubled over on the cot. She had one good pillow case which she stuffed with rags to make a pillow. And there was one thin striped towel clean. How was she going to get all these sheets dry and back on the beds on laundry day when there were no extras, she worried. Then she remembered travelling Colonist across Canada a year ago, coping with blankets and pillows, food and utensils, sharing, sharing everything with strangers in such a small space. She would manage somehow.

When Agnes went up to bed, Jessie was asleep on the box at the foot of the bed, but Edward was waiting for Agnes. He would not have a street waif under his roof, he stormed. The boy could murder us all. Agnes said calmly it was not his roof, it was Arnold's. And if Arnold brought a friend home, it was his house to do as he chose. Edward stormed on, but he heard what Agnes was saying and real-ized he had no power in Canada.

Deborah and Miriam were sharing a double bed in their room. When they heard their parents quarrelling again, with strangers in the house, they were embarrassed.

"And what about our Jessie?" Deborah said. "She's in there listening to all that rot."

"I wonder how long these young men will stay?" Miriam said.

"I hope forever," Deborah began to laugh, and they ducked under the covers to have a giggle. "I like that Louis."

When they surfaced, Miriam said, "We've got to get our sister out of there. Suppose she wakes up while they are at it?"

"Oh, they'll have given that up long ago," Deborah said. "They fight like cats and dogs."

"That wouldn't stop them making up under the covers. Suppose our mother became pregnant at the age of fifty-two."

"We could put an announcement in *The Leader.*"

"Fifty-two-year-old woman gives birth to a child with a beard on Twelfth Avenue."

They ducked under the covers again.

When they surfaced Miriam said, "Now seriously, Deborah, what are we going to do about our Jessie? Why don't we bring her in here and put a bed against that wall."

"We have no more beds..."

"We won't tell Mother. We'll meet in Victoria Square after work and bring home one of those canvas army cots. Then we'll just move her bedding in here and not say a word."

They did. They also prepared Jessie for "the curse," knowing their mother would not.

For the week after the cyclone the short round figure with the heavy walk could be seen carrying baskets of food to the tent community in Victoria square. Agnes would take home first one then another of the homeless women for a bath and a change of clothing.

Within two days Regina was a city of hammering. Arnold worked evenings after his regular job at the hardware store. Billy was paid to dig graves and bury the dead. Edward, age sixty-two, found work as a carpenter. His spirits lifted with earning some cash. He stopped complaining about the household arrangements – he now rather enjoyed the extra company. It reminded him of his childhood – his parents could afford to entertain. Since he had married, since he lost his inheritance in a fire, he had been too poor. The family had had to hide their poverty. But now these young men brought outside life into the family, and they paid for their keep.

CHAPTER 6

July 17, 1912

When Agnes Jackson sat at her dinner table that Saturday evening, she did not realize she had, in the past month, slid into the working class despite her long struggle to cling to the respectability of the lower middle class. What she did realize was that she had become the head of the table to a large, conversational family, and she was fulfilled. She had always been the one to carve the roast or fowl and apportion the meat helpings, but to a silent Edward, a silent Arnold, and nervous chatter from the three girls, nervous that they would be corrected for their table manners – *"Don't reach," "Don't point."*

Agnes glanced around at her new family members. Louis, the lively Welsh gentleman who worked at The Glasgow House in Men's Furnishings. He brought laughter with him into the house. He was now tittering across the table with Deborah as to who could find the greatest number of shot pellets in the prairie chickens the men had brought home and Agnes had cleaned and roasted. Louis and Deborah both had pale brown eyes, but Louis's were larger and heavily lashed, which made the upper part of his face look serious. Deborah lifted her face and rested it on her closed hand as she teased him, to show off the three dimples in her chin. Jessie quoted her mother, "Deborah, Deborah, strong and able, take your elbows off the table." Both parents frowned at her, not at Deborah.

Charles, the polite gentleman from Ontario, with his Roman nose, his fair hair cut so short. The son of an Anglican clergyman in Kingston, Ontario, he worked at the Northern Crown bank. He wore Harris tweed jackets that the girls complained smelled of sheep's urine when he got soaked in a rainstorm, but his boots were always polished, as were Arnold's.

And Billy, that compact Dr. Barnardo's boy, who had a ravenous appetite and spoke not at all, but watched everything. There had been an unpleasant incident with Billy the first breakfast when he answered "Nowt" to Agnes. Jessie repeated the sound, mocking him. Deborah laughed. Jessie was sent to eat in the kitchen.

Agnes was grateful for Billy. He got up at five when she did to empty the ashes and stoke the furnace and her cookstove. He chopped kindling and carried wood and the coal scuttle up from the basement. And he stayed clean. Arnold had introduced him to the bath tub, and Deborah had trained him to clean and cut his nails with the nail file and scissors left in the bathroom cupboard. Miriam had given him a jar of vaseline for his lips, but it did not heal the chronic split in his lower lip. Arnold had cut his thick mat of hair and bought him a hair brush, a tooth brush, and a shaving brush. Arnold taught him to use all three. Charles had found him a job replanting Dutch elm trees in the parks and along the streets. On Sundays before breakfast Arnold took Billy and Louis shooting prairie chickens, grouse, and jack rabbits.

All three of the new men paid board to her, Agnes, not

Edward – the same money as they had paid at the YMCA and restaurants – but here, they claimed, they ate spendidly, and spirits were high. So Agnes was able to hire Julia, a young Romanian from the east side of town, to do the washing and cleaning. Jessie loved Julia. She followed her into the basement, watching her spread Fels Naphtha soap over the rough surface of the washboard before she scrubbed the clothes. Jessie turned the mangle, then handed Julia clothes pins when she hung out the clothes. The towels Julia spread on the bushes to dry. After Julia had ironed the clothes, Jessie helped her fold the sheets and towels and remake the beds. They dusted and waxed together. When Julia was doing down the stairs, Jessie positioned herself in the downstairs hall so she could examine Julia's many ruffled petticoats and lace-trimmed knickers. She would wear those when she grew up.

Arnold had avoided Jack Foxxe after the cyclone. Since Louis and Charles had moved in, Arnold enjoyed their company more than Jack's. They seemed men of substance in their different ways, whereas Jack seemed hollow. But Jack seem impervious to Arnold's disapproval, to forget Arnold's anger that he had tried to renege on their agreement about building this house and the one next door. Arnold had been brought up with his mother's stricture that a man's word was a good as his bond. Perhaps she meant a gentleman, and Jack was a scallawag. Yet Arnold needed Jack. He wanted to continue to build houses – it was what he most enjoyed doing – and he needed Jack, not as a partner, but as a contact. Jack knew the real estate market, and his father was on City Council.

If Jack needed company, he sought Arnold out. He turned up one afternoon with a bouquet of flowers for Agnes. He was invited to stay for dinner. He began coming for dinner on Saturday and Sunday evenings. He again brought flowers to Agnes, which flustered her. It was one more thing to deal with when she was making dinner. After that, Louis suggested quietly to Jack that the others paid twenty-five cents for their meals. Jack tried to pay more, but Agnes would not have it.

Agnes was pleased to see Arnold chuckle and talk at table. As a child, he had been a chuckler, a happy child. When did that stop? Was it when his brother Stanley died? Or was it just the hard times that hit the family?

Even Edward seemed to be following the conversation, but only occasionally did he speak. The first week they had added constantly to information about the devastation of the storm. Louis was referring to the storm as a cyclone, as most Reginans did.

Edward spoke. "Why do you call it a cyclone?"

Louis looked alarmed. Agnes and Arnold sent angry glances at Edward. The girls exchanged expressions of exasperation. But Charles, the quiet one, said, "Mr. Jackson is right to query the use of the word cyclone. *The Leader* says a tornado is a local whirlwind of extreme violence usually found within a thunderstorm. That's what I hear we experienced. I'm sure that's what you saw across the lake, Arnold."

Deborah looked across the table at Charles and smiled.

"And experienced it too at the lake," Arnold retorted. "Those three minutes felt like three hours."

Charles went on, "A cyclone on the other hand is an atmospheric system where the pressure is lowest at the centre and the winds rotate spirally with a general rapid advance, like eddies in a swift stream."

Louis looked crushed and Edward's mouth widened to a near smile. He turned his grey eyes on Charles. He did not expect a Canadian to be well-informed.

Charles had more to say. "Both these descriptions tally more or less with that of Regina's storm. That of the tornado tallies more exactly."

That pronouncement was a conversation stopper. Louis looked around. What could he say for fun after such a lecture?

Agnes filled in. "I had a friend drop in for lunch yesterday," she said. The others looked expectantly at her. "I was sitting at the kitchen table eating bread and dripping with a cup of tea, when an Indian woman walked in the back door and sat at the table with me. So I poured her a cup of tea and cut a slice of bread and spread it with dripping. I think she said her name was Sulee, or some such. I gave her my name, then we chatted, each in our own language. After she had eaten, she shook my hand and walked out the door. What do you make of that, Charles?" Agnes would not have dared tell this incident to Edward or Arnold without the others present.

"I would have been scared," Jessie said.

That was what Agnes had first felt, but she would not admit it.

"Oh, there's no need to be scared," Charles said. "The Indians have a...well, more civilized attitude to the earth's gifts. Things belong to the Great Spirit. What we have, we share. Of course with our concept of private property, so many Indians end up in jail when they take what they need. They don't take more."

"Well," Louis said, slapping his hands on the table. "Anyone for a singsong?" He looked at Deborah.

The young people gathered around the piano, Louis and Miriam playing. Miriam had been "put to the piano" because she couldn't hold a tune like Deborah. Deborah was already in the choir of St. Paul's Church. She stood by the piano, a slight figure in her brown voile dress with the lace V neck. She sang her favourite song, *"I love life, I want to live, to drink of life's fullness and take all it can give."* Her mother was in the kitchen washing up, wishing they would sing hymns instead, but assuming no harm was being done. She was pleased to hear Arnold's baritone in full voice. She loved hearing him as a boy, when his father wasn't home, bellowing *"Wider still and wider, shall thy bounds be set, God, who made thee mighty, make thee mightier yet!"*

Louis was enchanted by Deborah singing *"I love life."* He had not heard that song before. Charles was also enchanted by Deborah and by the sense of the song, if not the sentimentality.

Louis seemed to reply to Deborah by singing

Believe me if all those endearing young charms
Which I gaze on so fondly today
Were to change by tomorrow and fade in my arms
Like fairy gifts fading away
Thou would still be adored, as this moment thou art
Let thy loveliness fade as it will
And around the dear ruin, each wish of my heart
Will entwine itself verdantly still

Charles envied Louis's tenor voice, his ability to woo a woman with song. Louis's voice mellowed into a Welsh accent when he sang and the first syllable of "verdantly" rhymed with "air" which Charles liked so much more than the flat Canadian "vur." And Louis seemed able to play by ear. Charles's mother had laughed that Charles seemed to be tone deaf, so he had always sung softly. The thought of his mother and her scorn that he was not other than he was upset him. He went out into the back garden where Edward

Jackson was checking his hens, his geese, his vegetables. Edward reached under a hen and handed Charles a warm egg. "Here's summat for your breakfast," he said

Charles was pleased, and wondered if Edward had noticed himself slipping into dialect.

Edward found two more eggs which he cradled as he walked among his plants, picking peas and beans and tucking them into a cotton sack on his arm. When he turned to go back in the house, Charles followed him. He would have liked to stay longer in the garden, golden in the evening sun, but he sensed that this was Edward's space, and he must be careful not to intrude. There were so many of them packed into this small house, of which Edward must be titular head. Did he resent the crowding the tornado had forced on him?

In the kitchen Agnes reached for a pencil and wrote C on the egg that Charles gave her. "How would you like it cooked for breakfast?" she asked.

"Oh, always boiled, thank you, Mrs. Jackson."

Charles rejoined the young. Louis was singing a new song – "*If I were the only boy in the world.*" Then he led them in singing "*Just a song at twilight*" and "*Home Sweet Home.*"

An air of melancholy floated through the room. They stopped singing. Where was home? Were they home? If so, how long would it last?

CHAPTER 7

November 1, 1912

Winter closes in on Regina in late October or early November. A blizzard, the temperature drops to below zero, the days shorten, snow banks halt traffic, and Wascana Lake freezes over. In the dark winter evenings the young people skated on the lake. Charles taught them to play hockey.

When they came home the first night about nine o'clock Charles looked in the kitchen for a cup of tea. Jessie was sitting in the rocking chair, a pair of scissors in her hand. She was cutting raisins into quarters for the Christmas mincemeat. Agnes sat on a straight chair at the wooden table, a Mrs.Beaton cookbook propped in front of her. At her feet was a ceramic crock into which she had already put currants, chopped apples, suet, and chopped oranges and lemons. She was cutting candied orange peel and lemon peel.

"Why don't you come skating, poppet?" Charles asked Jessie.

Jessie looked at her mother. "I haven't any skates." She longed to be sailing into the vast white on a pair of skates. She wanted to learn to play hockey.

"Well, that won't do. Here you are in Canada, and you aren't skating."

"She must wait until Christmas and see what Father Christmas brings her," Agnes said.

"Christmas is a long time off. Why don't you and I shop for skates tomorrow after I finish work, Jessie? That will be my Christmas present early. Is that all right with you, Mrs. Jackson?"

Jessie gave a rare smile, looking down.

Agnes began grating a nutmeg into her crock. No, it wasn't all right. It would be good for the child to do without, to wait until Christmas for things. But she dared not challenge Charles. She counted on the money her boarders brought in. She mustn't offend him.

Christmas at the Jacksons' was much different from what Charles had grown up with. It was an exuberant celebration. Mrs. Jackson and the girls had covertly knitted, sewn and cooked through October, November, and December. Much was hidden in trunks in the basement and under the girls' beds. The cold pantry had filled up with light Christmas cakes and dark Christmas cakes, puddings, pans of white and dark fudge, Turkish Delights, shortbread cut in wedges, and mince tarts by the dozen.

On December first Louis pasted Advent calendars to the living room and dining room windows. Jessie awoke to the sleigh bells of the milkman. Each morning when she got up, she and Billy opened an advent window. In the evenings when they weren't skating or attending Christmas music concerts at churches, the young sang Christmas carols around the piano. A week before Christmas Louis and

Arnold bought a fir tree from the Coast. Louis hung a mistletoe in the hall doorway so that he could catch and kiss the girls. Agnes unpacked a box of holly and cedar boughs sent from her sister on the Coast. Agnes tucked them in the plate rack, over pictures and among plates of cakes, pies, candies and nuts that she left on the sideboard for snacks. The house smelled of fir and cedar and sausage rolls baking. Tree ornaments were brought home and silver tinsel and icicles. Jessie and Billy tried to involve everyone in decorating the tree, but Agnes and Edward sat back and watched. The week before Christmas presents wrapped in red and green tissue paper began to appear under the tree, until by Christmas Eve the living room was impassable with the mountain of presents.

Yet Deborah announced, as she did every year, "You'll just have to have Christmas without me. I can't possibly get ready." She was wrapping presents on the ironing board. No one was supposed to look, but Jessie had to.

Christmas Eve, apart from Edward and Arnold, they trudged out in the crisp dark and sparkling snow to midnight carol service at their two churches.

Christmas morning a stocking hung at the fireplace for everyone, stuffed with a Brazil nut, a Japanese orange, wrapped candies, and something useful. Agnes served tea and warm buttered Welsh cakes as they sat around the tree. Then Arnold was assigned to be Father Christmas, to read the labels on presents and pass them out. The air resounded with exclamations of surprise and kisses. "Just what I wanted! Thank you." Billy had wrapped for each of the others bars of chipped soap which he got free from the Young-Thomas Soap Company, where he had found a winter job. Agnes had, on four steel needles, knitted socks for the men, gloves for the girls. Jessie, on large wooden kneedles, had knitted in the garter stitch, mufflers for all. Charles, as well as the skates, gave Jessie a pair of beaded moccasins for walking in the snow, and to Edward he gave Havana cigars. The older girls received silk stockings and scarves; the men boxed handkerchiefs and fudge and Turkish delights made by the girls. Agnes received a tea set of Japanese china from the girls, and chocolates from Louis, but what moved her most was a copy of *Adam Bede* from Charles, who had noticed how like Mrs. Poyser she was.

Billy crumpled the tissue paper into the fireplace. He got dry kindling from the basement and frosty wood from the back porch. Agnes gave him one cedar bough from the Coast to lay under the wood, as it was beginning to dry in the central heating, and might cause a fire.

At lunchtime sausage rolls were warmed and served with olives, celery, Christmas cake and coffee. The family had to eat in the cluttered living room, for Agnes had set the table for dinner with the lace cloth and sterling silver she had inherited from her mother. She had placed red tapers in four silver candle sticks, and a pyramid of Japanese oranges in a cut glass bowl as her centrepiece. Christmas crackers waited on the white linen napkins at each place.

The girls had vegetable chores in the kitchen. By five o'clock the house smelled of sage and sausage stuffing, and roasted turkey sent from the farm by Aunt Fannie and Uncle George. The candles were lit, the men seated. The girls paraded in with bowls filled with potatoes, brussel sprouts, carrots, peas, sweet potatoes, creamed onions, and gravy. Then Agnes came in to cheers, carrying high the eighteen-pound turkey on a platter. She sat. Edward intoned grace, "For what we are about to receive may the Lord make us truly thankful, for Christ's sake, Amen."

The crackers were pulled and coloured tissue crowns

put on heads. Deborah began to read aloud the fortune that came inside her cracker, but Agnes, carving, interrupted. "Save that nonsense until later and get it into you while it's hot. Jessie, I've forgotten the cranberry sauce in the cold pantry. Miriam, the bread sauce is still in the double boiler. Put it in the warm sauce dish above the stove."

The Christmas pudding had a different entrance from the turkey. The electric lights were turned off. Brandy was poured over the pudding, and lit to produce a blue flame as the pudding was carried in, a sprig of holly in its center. Agnes liked a cream sauce with it, flavored with almond, but she also had made a hard buttery sauce with brandy. Jessie and Billy were somehow served the coins wrapped in waxed paper and hidden in the pudding. After pudding, figs and dates were put on the table, and bowls of nuts with nut crackers and picks. Arnold produced a bottle of port. Not looking at his mother, he went to the sideboard and found his grandmother's crystal wine glasses for the men. The girls demanded a glass too, but Agnes, being a member of the Women's Christian Temperance Union, shook her head.

After dinner the girls cleared the table and the men washed up. Agnes sat by the fire with her book opposite Edward in his chair, who had begun reading *The Last Days of Pompeii*, given to him by Arnold. When the washing up was done, Jessie brought out cards for a noisy game called "Pit." The young sat around the dining table shouting and groaning until Deborah changed the game to Musical Chairs. They took the leaves out of the dining table, pushed it back and lined up the chairs. Miriam played while the others marched, Deborah and Louis landing often on each other's laps. They played Charades, acting out scenes in front of the parents until Deborah and Jessie began to argue, and Miriam moved them to the piano to sing carols. Agnes sang with them.

The mantle clock struck midnight. Christmas Day was over.

When Agnes and Edward went up to bed, Edward said, "Well done, Agnes!" as he used to say when they were first married. In bed he cuddled up to her and held her until she fell into her usual deep sleep.

CHAPTER 8

December 26, 1912

Agnes took Boxing Day off. She put out corn flakes and prunes and bread and let the young make their own breakfasts. She had beef and barley soup made from a shin of beef for lunch, and cold turkey and warmed up vegetables and pudding for dinner. The girls did the cooking and washing up. She sat with a pencil in "her" chair in the living room filling in the engagement calendar Arnold had given her with what she called "the tyranny of meals." August and September she blocked in with pickling and preserving, and November with Christmas baking. She called out to Louis and Charles and Billy asking their birthdays. When Billy mumbled, she said, "Well, we'll give you July second. That's the important day you came to us, and we have no July birthdays except for Canada."

For birthdays Agnes usually made a sponge cake. She wrapped coins in waxed paper and slid them into the cake so that each member of the family would get a surprise. Then she iced the cake with a lemon icing and topped it with candles which she lit in the kitchen. Meanwhile one of the girls would turn the lights off, and Agnes would enter to the singing of *"Happy Birthday."* She would try to cook the birthday person's favourite meal, and despite Jessie's complaints, she also made a jelly mould, which she served with fresh custard when the hens were laying, or Devonshire cream when it was winter. Presents wrapped in white and pink tissue paper were opened by the fireplace.

Jessie's would be the first birthday, New Year's Day. Agnes scratched her head with the pencil. She liked to cook a goose for New Year's Day, but she could see that Edward was so attached to his two geese, now in the basement, that he would be upset if she wanted to kill one. She decided to cook a roast of pork, roasted potatoes, and she had a few apples left to make applesauce. For dessert she had a second Christmas pudding steamed. She would put the coins in that and the candles on top, then there would be no noise from Miss Fussy about jelly for birthdays.

Working back, what would she serve New Year's Eve? The young would want to celebrate. She would make just a macaroni cheese for dinner with cole slaw, then make a fruit punch to serve at midnight with all the baking left over from Christmas. The men seemed to like her mince tarts. She would heat those up. Who could be the tall dark man to knock on the door at midnight with a lump of coal for luck in the New Year? Arnold would be the logical one, he was taller than Louis, but would he? If not, Louis would have to do. Was that before or after they sang *"Auld Lang Syne,"* their joined hands raised and lowered, raised and lowered? Agnes dozed off, her engagement calendar on her lap. She did not hear the young troop out, skates over their shoulders.

CHAPTER 9

January 3, 1913

Arnold Jackson had been given the sack. Mr. Dowswell, the junior partner, had assured Arnold that it was not that his work was unsatisfactory – it was this damned recession. Now that the railroad was completed, and what with the crop failure last year, sales were down and Arnold was the last to be hired. But they liked his work. Arnold took his pay, bought a *Leader*, and went to the Elite Cafe. He ordered a coffee and lit a Sweet Caporal.

When he opened the newspaper to the Classified ads, there it was again: *No Englishmen need apply*. When he first arrived in Regina in June of 1909, it was there in store windows and classified ads. Arnold had been so frightened by the message that he had continued on to his uncle and aunt's farm at Gibbs. He had no money to get back to England, where he had had a job in an iron-monger's. Other men in the Colonist Car of the train across Canada were going to farm. One could get a quarter section of land free by building a house on it and occupying it. He would farm.

June 1910, Gibbs, Saskatchewan

There was one thing worse than having no money in Regina. That was to try to farm with no money. Arnold's uncle George, over six feet tall, met Arnold at the station with a horse and Red River cart borrowed from a neighbour. He and Aunt Fannie were living in a sod hut they had built themselves from the thick pelt of grasses they had had to break before they could plant a garden. The house sagged and weeds flowered over its surface. Arnold was expected to sleep on the earth floor on some straw in this one room with his aunt and uncle, who slept in a bed with dirty sheets. The room smelled acrid from chicken droppings. Arnold was appalled. Agnes had kept such a clean, well-run house, and was always well-groomed. Tiny Aunt Fannie – well, what could she do? She had only two upper teeth left, and those her canines. "We've had to live like animals," she smiled ruefully at Arnold. "My father would be so upset."

Water was drawn in a bucket from a well. They washed in an enamel basin set on a wooden orange box outside the door. The privy was a pit dug in nearby poplar scrub, with two poles propped above it. Arnold found another growth of scrub and created a bed. Aunt Fannie let him take a quilt out there. The first night coyotes howled and he wondered if he were going to have to dash to the sod hut, but they seemed more afraid of him than he them. He had bought a shotgun in Regina. He shot jackrabbits instead of coyotes, which Aunt Fannie stewed.

The weather at first was tolerable. He had yet to experience the heat of a prairie summer or the cold of a prairie winter. Fannie and George had survived the winter in that hut, sharing it with the chickens and a cow. Uncle George had been a coachman in England, his skill not needed with the arrival of horseless carriages. He knew nothing about farming or building. The warmth of the cow had helped to keep them from freezing, and they burned its dung. The nearest neighbours, the Renwicks and Fishers, had sold them the milking cow and given them some chicks to raise, so that they at least had milk, eggs, and the occasional chicken.

When Arnold appeared for breakfast the first morning Thomas Renwick had come over with his team of horses and stone sled. He had decided that Arnold would help clear ten acres of stones so that Uncle George could plant grain in the black loam. Clearing stones was back-breaking work. Then Renwick organized the neighbours to raise the frame of a small house for them. He directed George and Arnold how to roof it with flattened kerosene cans and to hammer tar paper on the walls. It was hot work. Arnold dug a root cellar for the vegetables Auntie Fannie had planted. As there was no slough on the property, Thomas Renwick insisted Arnold also dig a fourteen foot dugout so that melting snow would become water for cattle, and help to produce rain. "When you've got water, you get water," he claimed.

By September the tarpaper shelter was the house and the sod hut was a barn. Arnold, ten pounds lighter, fled back to Regina.

September 1910, Regina, Saskatchewan

Arnold found lodgings in Osler Street. The other young men staying in the house were English settlers also looking for work. It was discouraging company.

Sunday morning Arnold went to church for something to do. He chose his mother's church – the Methodists – because in England they were friendlier. The Anglicans pretended you were not there. It was a good choice. At the end of the service, there was a lineup of welcoming members who shook his hand and urged him to join the choir or the Men's Club. At the end of the line a handsome young man with brown hair slicked back kept shaking his hand and smiling but saying nothing. Finally he said, "Do you smoke?"

"Yes." Arnold brought his Turrets out of his pocket.

"Not here, not here. Someone might see." He looked up the receiving line. "Would you like to take a stroll around the square? Or better still, we could go down on the lake. My family has a rowboat down there."

Jack Foxxe was the son of a local developer. He had just finished high school, and didn't want to go East to a university as his friends had done. He didn't have the marks or the interest. His father was making him work in the family business, which Jack hated.

Arnold had not seen Wascana Lake before. A large structure was going up across the lake. "The Legislative Buildings," Jack said.

In the rowboat they exchanged cigarettes. Jack introduced Arnold to Sweet Caporals.

"So what do you want to do?" Arnold asked Jack. He stretched back, his hat brim over his eyes against the September sun.

"I'd like to canoe across Canada," Jack said.

"But realistically. To earn your living."

"Men used to do that, you know, to earn a living. Canoe across Canada, trade in furs, marry Indian girls."

Arnold envied this young man the luxury of being lost, of not having to earn money to survive.

"Yes, but I'm not sure that's one of your options in 1910."

"You sound like my father. And until I can decide what to do I have to work for him. And I don't like my father. Or

50

my mother either for that matter."

Arnold felt he had found a kindred spirit. He disliked his parents too.

"So what does your father do? What does he expect you to do?"

"Oh, he buys up land cheap and puts houses on it. Now he's working on that structure over there." Jack waved at the Legislative Building. "What does he expect me to do? For one thing, join churches and clubs so I can sell his houses for him. That's why I was in that line-up today. And politics. He says it's important to contribute to both political parties, so that whoever wins has to give you contracts or benefits of some kind."

Arnold whistled under his breath and watched the oars dip in the water. So that's the way the new world worked. Or the old world too. Only he hadn't known.

"What about you?" Jack asked. "What do you do?"

Arnold smiled at the question. What did he do, indeed? He said he was a tinsmith, that is, he worked in an iron-monger's in England, a hardware store here. So he was looking for work in a hardware store.

"A man who lives next to us owns a hardware store. We give him all our business. Would you like me to ask him for a job for you?"

Arnold was given the job of drayman, driving the delivery cart for Armstrong, Smyth and Dowswell. He picked up the large boxes at the railway station from wholesalers back east, and restocked the shelves. He also made deliveries within the city.

One evening – it was an Indian summer – Jack showed him a lot on 12th Avenue that his father had given him to build on. Basements had been dug for two houses.

"But it's only fifty feet wide," Arnold said. "The bylaws won't allow two houses on it."

"My father's now a city councillor," Jack said. "His employees won't question anything he owns."

Jack asked Arnold to borrow the hardware's cart and horse to haul left-over lumber from the Legislative Buildings. Jack's father also had command of that.

With the fine lumber on site, Jack wanted to start building. "Help me," he said to Arnold.

Arnold had learned carpentry from his father in the house in Manchester, and the basics of house raising from Thomas Renwick at Gibbs, but not for a house with a full basement. The room at Gibbs had only a crawl space. "You'll have to pay me," he said, conscious of the difference in their standards of living.

Jack thought. His father expected him to work on the site himself, to cut corners when it came to hiring. "Look," he said, "why don't we build the one house, sell it, and with the money hire someone to build the second house. Then I'll give you one of the houses as payment."

"That's generous. Agreed," Arnold said. He made Jack shake hands on the deal. The snow came and filled the excavation and covered the lumber for the winter. Arnold spent his spare time in the library studying books on construction.

The first house sold before it was finished in July, 1911. Jack had not worked on site. He hired unemployed men to help Arnold, and had organized the supplies. Arnold assumed there would now be money free to hire skilled tradesmen to make his life simpler, but when Jack drove up in a new Model T, Arnold sensed trouble. Jack seemed to have forgotten the agreement that Arnold was to have the second house built in payment for his work on the first. When Arnold insisted he remember, Jack backed off and agreed that 2929 was Arnold's payment, but he had already invested the money from the first house in the car and another lot, assuming Arnold would keep building for him. Arnold said he would wait and see, but he now didn't trust Jack's word. *He's out to skin others. I should have been warned when he accepted his father bending the rules in his direction.* Dislike coursed through Arnold as he watched Jack drive off. *That's my car, brother. I paid for it with my labour.* But his family had arrived from England and were in lodgings in Osler Street. He had to find shelter for them in a city where housing was at a premium. He came straight from work at the hardware store and spent the long summer evenings and all day Sunday on the 2929 site.

One golden summer evening Edward appeared with Arnold's supper. Arnold was in need of a helper to lift and place a floor beam. Edward put down the food and took the other end of the beam. He stayed clearing and sorting lumber and nails. The next evening he appeared with a carpenter's apron on. The house was finished before the snow fell in October.

January 3, 1913

Arnold lit another Sweet Cap. He had taken a mortgage on his house to cover his bills at the lumber yard. How was he going to meet those payments? How would he face his mother, who would have to feed him? He wondered if she got enough money from the others to cover the mortgage. After all, it was in all their interests to have a roof over their heads.

Arnold was not the only one to lose his job. Deborah

had been laid off from the Regina Trading Company.

"That's it," Agnes announced at table. "It's business school for you, Madam. Girls should have skills just as boys have."

And what skills did you pay for me to get, Madam? Arnold asked his mother in his head. He dared not look at his father. *He's so high and mighty. Why isn't he out working to support his family?*

Miriam and Louis seemed secure at The Glasgow House, which was surviving the recession. And Charles had been promoted to an accountant with the bank. After the clean-up work from the cyclone and tree planting had ended, Charles had got Billy a job in the Young-Thomas Company, a local firm making soap. Billy wasn't making much money, but he paid his board. Charles did the arithmetic – so of the nine of them around the table, four of them were working. They should manage. Not in the style of his mother in Kingston, Ontario, who kept a maid, but Mrs. Jackson was a good manager. He wouldn't be surprised if she had money set by for a rainy day.

CHAPTER 10

March 24, 1913

Jessie sat in the kitchen rocking chair to read to her mother, who was making tripe and onions.

"'1000 Facts About Regina, Saskatchewan' from *Canada's City of Certainties*, 1912. Regina has the following, among many other stores:

40 grocery
12 drug
10 bake shops

"Mother, why can't we buy bread at a bake shop instead of eating what you bake all the time?

17 restaurants.

"Why can't we eat in a restaurant some of the time?"

Agnes gashed her thumb trying to cut the gristle off a large piece of tripe. Damson blood spurted onto the white meat, settling in the waffling of its underside. "Go and get the rag bag," Agnes said. When Jessie brought it, Agnes pointed out a worn pillow case. "Now, tear a strip off that, there's a girl, then tear the end for about an inch. Now wind the other end tight around my thumb, and tie it. Now cut the ends off so that it doesn't get into the food. Well done."

Agnes moved to the sink and ran the cold tap. "Now, hold that end of the meat so we can rinse the blood out of it. It's supposed to be white. I'll keep my thumb in the air."

Jessie held her end of the waffled cow's stomach and said, "Ugh! That stuff looks awful!"

"You've never been hungry, that's your problem, madam. Waste not, want not. Now get on with your reading."

3 furniture stores
14 butchers
6 booksellers
9 boot and shoes
12 gents' furnishings
20 ice cream and confectionery

"Mother, why can't we..."
"Now just get on with your reading, Miss Greedy."

4 hardware stores
7 printers
10 barber shops
10 billiard and pool
12 blacksmith shops
2 greenhouses
1 steam laundry
15 hand laundries
8 liveries
7 lumber yards

700 drays
14 architectural firms
19 legal firms
9 dentists
29 physicians

"Mother what is a dentist?"

"Oh, it's a man you go to when you get a toothache. He pulls it out."

"And physicians?" She stumbled for a second time over the word.

"Oh, those are doctors."

Jessie began to cry. "You shouldn't have let him in the house. You shouldn't have let him do it."

Agnes wiped her hands on her apron, and put them on Jessie's shoulders. Jessie had had her tonsils snipped out on the kitchen table by the doctor before the family left England.

"There, there. It's over now. We didn't want you to get the diphtheria that took our poor Stanley, did we?"

But Agnes shared Jessie's pain and doubts. Why had she let him do it without anaesthetic? It seemed a brutal attack on a child.

At the dinner table, when she served the tripe and onions, Charles looked at his plate. His pale skin grew green. He ate the potatoes and turnip mashed in with the carrots, but left the meat dish.

Agnes had had this out with the children in England. Edward didn't approve of children refusing food. He would send them from the table. But what about boarders? "You don't like tripe and onions, after all my trouble?" She had a coal smut on her left temple, most unusual for Agnes. She also had a bandaged thumb.

"I must confess I've never tried it. But I have a weak stomach."

Louis and Arnold laughed.

"There's some leftover roast mutton in the cold pantry. Shall I get it?" Jessie asked.

"Why don't we go out to a restaurant?" Deborah asked. "There's a new one opened called The Maple Leaf."

Agnes's cheeks flamed. She would lose her boarders if they started going out to restaurants. She couldn't have that. She got up and brought the remains of the roast mutton, the carving knife, some mint sauce, and a clean plate from the kitchen.

"Oh please don't bother," Charles said. "I can fill up on bread."

But Agnes didn't hear him. When she asked who else wanted cold roast, everyone but Edward had some. When she served Jessie a small portion she couldn't help saying, as if to the whole table, "Your eyes are bigger than your stomach, Madam."

"Louis has invited me to the R.H. Williams dance at the City Hall," Deborah announced. She turned to Miriam, who worked in the office of the R.H. Williams Glasgow House. "Can you make me a gown if I bring the material home?"

"Yes," Miriam said, dismayed that she had not been invited to her own firm's dance. She stood and took dishes into the kitchen. Over the sink she looked in the small mirror. Was she too tall to get a boy friend? Would she never marry?

Arnold, sensing Miriam's hurt, followed her into the kitchen. She was the reflective one in the family. She thought before she spoke. The other two had rattling tongues.

"May I have the honour of escorting you to the dance, Miss?" Arnold asked of Miriam's back. She turned to him and smiled. He was still half in love with this beautiful sister with her olive skin and thick dark hair.

A t the dance, which was held nearby in the City Hall, Jack Foxxe cut in the first dance Arnold had with Miriam. He was as tall as Miriam, with regular features, and he was a good dancer. Miriam and Jack danced most of the evening together. She liked his flickering smile, the sight of his small overlapping teeth through thin tight lips. But she also saved dances for Arnold.

Arnold went upstairs to the balcony, lit a cigarette, and looked down on the dancers. He wasn't pleased to see Jack make such a fuss of Miriam, the handsomest girl in the room. And there was no sense in his looking around, there was such a shortage of girls in Regina. He did not cut a dashing figure like Jack. His face looked like a boiled pudding when he looked in the mirror. And he had no prospects, despite getting his job back at the hardware, and a promotion to the sales staff. Yes, now he could wear a business suit and a fedora – better than a cloth cap. But marriage was out of the question.

C harles Wilson had never learned to dance. His father, like Edward's, was an Anglican clergyman. Charles took a second chair out on the verandah and sat by Edward, who offered him part of the *Manchester Guardian*. Charles sensed that Edward, like him, was timid out in the world. He would not, like Louis, have played rugby on the street or on the village green, not have had children in to play, not have played much at all. So much of life in a clergyman's family was concerned with appearances and what was acceptable behaviour. Charles's family never laughed. He suspected that Edward's family had not laughed either. He felt comfortable sitting on the verandah with this quiet man in this raw city with its mud streets and wooden sidewalks.

CHAPTER 11

Easter, 1913

On Good Friday the family, apart from Agnes and Billy, who had been up since daylight, awoke to the spicy smell of Hot Cross Buns baking. When Agnes brought the warm buns nestled in a striped tea towel in to the breakfast table, she sang, and her girls sang with her

Hot cross buns! Hot cross buns!
One a penny, two a penny
Hot cross buns!
If you have no daughters
Give them to your sons
One a penny, two a penny
Hot cross buns!

Charles was pleased, having grown up without such traditions. Agnes explained that Good Friday, after church attendance, was considered in England a blessed day to plant beans and parsley, the parsley seeds to be sown out of a steel thimble. Edward hadn't always used her steel thimble, a risk she wished he would take. And flowers seeds sown on Good Friday were expected to produce double flowers.

On Easter Sunday Deborah and Miriam wore new clothes to church. Agnes bought herself a scarf, hat and gloves. Jessie was allowed new shoes and gloves and stockings. Her dress, hat, and purse were hand-me-downs from both Miriam and Deborah. She and Billy got chocolate Easter eggs from all of the grown-ups.

Edward and Arnold did not go to church in Canada. Edward had been once to St. Paul's Anglican before deciding it was bad form evangelical. Arnold wanted whatever free time he had to himself. Billy did what Arnold did.

Louis and Charles, both with new ties, Charles with a new hat, walked the women along Twelfth Avenue towards Victoria Square. The melting snow made walking slippery, and created runnels under the wooden sidewalks. Louis and Agnes walked on to the Methodist Church. Charles, Deborah, and Miriam went into St. Paul's Anglican.

Arnold and Billy took Billy's football across the railroad tracks to the Exhibition Grounds. Billy had shown himself adept with footwork after Arnold and Louis had taken him to watch the Regina team. Arnold hoped that with practice Billy could try out for a local soccer team. Billy picked wild crocuses on the way home. He presented them to Agnes who put them in a dish on the dinner table. She had already put a bouquet of dandelions from Jessie in her low cut glass bowl at the center of the table.

Agnes had cooked a ham and a two-crust lemon pie the evening before. She had left a pan of scalloped potatoes baking in the oven. Always ham on Easter Day when they could afford it.

After Edward said grace, there was a knock on the door. Jessie skipped to the door and opened it. She gave a gasp they could hear in the dining room. Agnes rushed to the door. It was her younger brother Bob. Somehow his nose had collapsed, distorting his mouth, which had greyish sores on it. His thick lips were fissured, his hair had come out in patches. He had a tremor.

"Agnes?"

"Well, you'd best come in then." Agnes was less than gracious to have an extra mouth to feed, and what a mouth to sit with her boarders. She told him to put his suitcase in the hall. Then she took him upstairs to the bathroom and gave him a towel.

When she came back to the table, she said, "It's my brother Bob, come to make his fortune in Canada." She paused to let the irony sink in. "Jessie, you'd best set a place, and you sit on the kitchen stool, although he looks as if he's sick. Now eat up, the lot of you, or it will get cold."

Charles took one look at Bob, saw a very sick man, and helped Agnes make up a bed on the chesterfield. The next day he brought home another dining chair.

The whole household heard Edward and Agnes quarrelling in their room. The Jackson parents hadn't had a fight like this one since they left England. They resorted to their county dialects. Edward wanted Bob shipped off to Fannie's farm – he could work for his board there. Agnes argued that he was family, and families looked after one another. "After all, it could be you."

Edward was outraged at the thought. He went downstairs, put on his hat, took his cane, and walked on the prairie until it was dark.

CHAPTER 12

April 21, 1913

At dinner Jessie didn't want to eat her beef soup. Bob, who was improving with Agnes's good cooking, spoke up, his voice so slurred that it was difficult to understand him. "No broth, no ball. No ball, no beef." He struggled to smile that he could contribute. But Agnes was upset. Bob was quoting their father, and normally she would have been pleased to be reminded of her father's sayings. But in these hard times there was no way that she was going to serve three courses. The suet was in a marmalade pudding which was coming for dessert, with a custard sauce and tea. She could not serve dumplings as well. Bob slurped his tea, a practice Edward loathed. "When are you moving on?" he shouted across the table at Bob. Bob looked like a wild animal in a trap. He half stood and threw his cup of tea at Edward, splashing his beard and his vest.

"I don't have to put up with this in my own house!" Edward stood up. "Where's thy gun?" he turned to Arnold. Arnold was immobile, his knuckles grew white clutching the table. Edward got up and marched to the back hall where Arnold kept his guns.

Billy dived under the table.

"Quick, under the table," Charles said to the girls. He helped the girls under the table, then stood beside Agnes, who was leaning on the sideboard. Louis darted to the front hall. His voice could be heard phoning the police. Bob sat. Arnold sat across the table from him, feeling *Now it's going to happen. It's time.*

"Get down, Mr. Mitton. Get down Arnold," Charles ordered. But Bob did not understand what was happening and Arnold would not move.

The room exploded with the sound of the first shot. It glanced off the chandelier, scattering glass and flowers across the table. Charles opened his eyes as the second deafening shot hit Bob Milton. He gave a cry. Blood spurted out of him over the white table cloth.

It was Edward's turn to look bewildered. His ears were ringing, his arms sagged, but he still held the gun.

Two city police came. "No one move," they ordered as they entered the house. They looked at the slumped figure of Bob Mitton, then at Edward. "Phone for an ambulance," one said to Louis. Then they cajoled the shotgun away from Edward. "You come with us, sir." Agnes dashed ahead of them to the hall and produced Edward's coat and hat and cane. The police took Edward away.

Agnes walked past her injured brother and Arnold into the kitchen and closed the door. She sat in her rocking chair and rocked. Her world was collapsing again.

When the ambulance attendants arrived, Charles was staunching with a table napkin the flow of blood from a wound on Bob's shoulder. The room stank of sulpher. Louis was trying to comfort Deborah and Jessie who were crying. Billy, still under the table, was howling. Arnold and Charles helped to get Bob into the ambulance. When they came back,

Arnold shouted to Billy to stop the noise, it was all over. But he grizzled on under the table.

The others sat in silence on dining chairs, but away from the table, which was covered with glass.

"Where is she?" Arnold asked quietly.

Louis nodded towards the kitchen. Miriam went upstairs and came down with smelling salts. She gave a sniff to Deborah and Jessie, then knocked on the kitchen door and went in. In a few moments Agnes came back into the dining room. If she had been crying, no one could tell. Her face was a stoic mask. She lifted a corner of the white linen table cloth, noticing a blueing stain Julia hadn't washed out.

"Now, you, Billy, stop that grizzling and come up. I want to talk to all of you."

Billy scrambled up, his face swollen.

Agnes clenched her teeth, looking at each one of them. "We tell no one," she said. "We tell no one."

The next morning Arnold had to appear at the police headquarters to make a report. The officer in charge looked worried.

"What will be the charge?" Arnold asked.

"That depends on the medical reports. Your father will be detained here until we get them. Would you like to see him?"

"No," Arnold said, and walked out of the building.

Deborah went with Agnes to the Grey Nuns' Hospital to see Bob. He looked at Agnes, who held his hand in hers. He seemed afraid to talk.

"The doctor would like to see your son this afternoon if

he is free," a nurse said to Agnes.

On the walk home, Agnes began to fume. Why her son? Was she a non-person that she could not discuss her brother, her husband? After all, she was surely closer kin than Arnold.

Agnes pinned her cameo brooch on her best moiré dress and went with Arnold to meet the doctor.

"The gunshot wound is superficial, as you might guess," the doctor said to Arnold. He was a seedy young man with a greying beard. He wore a brown suit. "But your uncle has a more serious infection..." He looked at Agnes. "I'm afraid he hasn't long to live."

"It's consumption," Agnes announced. She began to worry about her daughters.

The doctor looked at Arnold again. "No, Mrs. Jackson. It's much more common than tuberculosis. It's syphilis. You can take him home probably tomorrow. He won't infect anyone."

Agnes stood. No one in her family had that disease.

"I am going to put on my medical report to the police that this man is an advanced case of syphilis, and that the gunshot wound was superficial."

Out in the street, when Agnes could find her voice, she said to Arnold, "We tell no one."

"Would you like to go for a cup of tea?" Arnold asked.

"No, I want to go home."

"Walk around the block with me. I have to think."

They circled a block of Rae Street before Arnold spoke. "The police will want Uncle Bob to lay a charge against Father. I think if they couldn't find him, they would have to drop the charges. I wonder if we could get him to the farm at Gibbs. After all, Auntie Fannie is his sister too."

Agnes stopped walking. She was shocked. The farm sounded such a primitive place to send a sick man.

"No, it's improved since I was there. Remember, every time Auntie Fannie writes they have some new comfort."

They were walking again. Now it was Arnold's turn to stop. "I could get a car from the livery and drive him up there straight from the hospital. Then no one need know where he is. He shouldn't come back to the house." He took Agnes's silence for agreement.

"What about your father?" she asked.

"Well, if the police can't find the evidence, they can't lay a charge," he guessed.

"I'll have to write to Fannie," Agnes said.

When Miriam got home, her mother was lying on the chesterfield under an afghan, and Deborah and Jessie were making dinner. Miriam got the news from them, then took a towel and a bottle of vaseline to the chesterfield. She undid her mother's stockings and took them off. Agnes wasn't asleep. She had just retreated into herself to absorb the tragedy that had befallen her. Miriam began massaging her mother's feet, something she had never done before. They were a family who didn't touch each other, except for the rare kiss on the cheek. But Miriam had long worried about her mother's swollen ankles. She massaged them upwards, wanting to reverse the flow of fluids that settled there, and restore the vital mother she remembered as a child. Miriam felt large callouses on the ball of each foot. She went for Arnold's razor in the basement and cut out the callouses. Agnes gave a sigh, as if the callouses had been pressing on nerves. Miriam massaged upwards again, but she could not move the fluid from her mother's ankles. She patted and covered her mother's feet.

While Arnold was driving Bob Mitton to Gibbs, Agnes turned her attention to her husband. She did not have Arnold's agreement to go to the Police Station. She went by herself. She missed Edward, despite their disagreements and this latest disgrace.

"He's gone," the duty policeman told her. "We took him by train this morning to North Battleford Provincial Hospital."

"Hospital? He's not sick."

"Doctor says he is."

"So why does he send him so far? Let me talk to the doctor."

There was no police doctor. They were using the seedy young man at Grey Nuns' Hospital who had looked after Bob. Agnes walked over to Grey Nuns' and asked to see the doctor. The nuns gave her a cup of tea while she waited.

The doctor told Agnes he had sent Edward to the Provincial Mental Hospital as he suspected he had a mental illness that caused the dangerous outburst of anger. "He doesn't belong in prison, an elderly gentleman like that," he said. "Up there he can be treated as a patient, not a criminal, and be seen by a psychiatrist. I am not one. We don't have one in Regina."

Agnes thought she said thank you as she stood up and left.

Blows, blows. When will life stop dealing me blows. What have I done to deserve this? she asked herself as she walked home. What to tell the others? How much to tell the others? Well, she would tell them Edward was in hospital at North Battleford – that was better than prison. They could draw their own conclusions. But what about Bob? She would tell them he died.

He did die. The drive to Gibbs over dry rutted prairie trails was too much for Bob Mitton. The first time Arnold stopped to change tires, his uncle was wheezing, green phlegm trickling from his nose. He wiped his uncle's face with a handkerchief and spoke to him, but the second time he stopped, Bob Mitton was dead of cardiovascular syphilis.

Arnold phoned his mother, who decided Bob should be buried in Gibbs, preferably on the farm. She sent money to Fannie and a handwritten quote from *Cymbeline* to be buried with Bob:

> *Fear no more the heat of the sun*
> *Nor the furious winter's rages*
> *Thou thy worldly task hast done*
> *Home art gone and ta'en thy wages*
> *Golden lads and girls all must*
> *As chimney sweepers, come to dust.*

CHAPTER 13

The Morning Leader, Regina, June 21, 1913

"With lights streaming from every window the handsome new Assiniboia Club presented a very festive appearance last night as throngs of guests arrived by motor and by carriage for the grand opening ball, one of the most brilliant and fashionable functions of the kind in the history of the capital."

Jessie studied her mother's feet and hands as she worked the new Singer Sewing Machine. Agnes had ripped thin sheets in half, and was sewing them together with the strong parts in the middle. Her feet rocked the treadle as her arms moved with the sheets away from her trunk. The fly wheel whirred. The needle did a clack-clack-clack. Jessie thought she would never be able to use a machine that went so fast. When her mother was out she had tried rocking the treadle. The clacking of the needle frightened her. Had she broken it?

"On with your reading, Miss. The devil makes work for idle hands."

"As the portals were thrown hospitably open the rotunda, banked with palms, was revealed, and just beyond, a glimpse of

the dining-room, the supper tables and buffet. Porters directed the ladies to the right, where in the dressing-rooms were to be found quantities of fragrant flowers and every convenience that thoughtfulness could provide. The lounge room on the main floor, in which a fire blazed and crackled in the great English fireplace, was used as a reception room. It was much regretted that the wife of the president, Mrs. Major Bishop, was unable through illness to receive with her husband, but her place as a hostess was graciously taken by Mrs. T.B. Patton, wife of the oldest member of the committee.

"Mrs. Patton was handsome in a gown of cream satin with back and front panel of pineapple cloth, hand embroidered in gold, and garniture of hand-made American silk lace. Her ornaments were cherry fire opals, and in her hair she wore a gold and cream band and aigrette."

"Ha! The smart set," Agnes said. "They make their money quickly and don't know how to spend it sensibly. Read on."

"After being announced and received, the guests were conducted to the second floor, where the spacious reading and writing rooms had been transformed into a ballroom. For those who preferred less strenuous amusement than dancing, there were four card rooms in which to arrange cosy games.

"Whebell's orchestra was stationed on the second landing, and, as always, provided a perfect programme of dance music.

"An elaborate and delicious supper was served from ten o'clock until one at quartette tables in the dining room, this long time being allotted to this important part of the programme to prevent crowding owing to the very large number present."

"Oh, stop that twaddle, and turn to The Glasgow House's sale page," Agnes said, not stopping sewing. Secretly she was enjoying the description of the Assiniboia

Club, for Miriam had gone to the opening ball with Jack Foxxe. Miriam had made herself a peach satin gown, which Agnes had beaded with small pearls. She had also lent Miriam her string of garnets and her garnet ring. Miriam had bought a white ostrich feather for her thick dark hair, which Agnes had curled with rags. And Miriam had bought a muskrat coat and muff on time from the Glasgow House. She did look handsome. And she did have a good time. But Jack didn't introduce Miriam to his parents, who were at the ball. "We're not good enough for them," Agnes realized.

Agnes didn't want to turn Jessie's head by having her read about balls. She was such a plain child, she would have to work hard all her life.

"What's this, Ma? *'Dr. Pierce's Golden Medical Discovery for Female Weakness – makes weak women strong, cures kindred ailments of women.'* What are kindred ailments, Ma? And this one, *'Lydia Pinkham's Vegetable Compound, the standard remedy for female ills.'* "

Agnes took pins from her mouth and stuck them in the piece of flannel she had wrapped around the body of the sewing machine.

"Stop the twaddle and turn to the Glasgow House page."

"Glasgow House: Thanksgiving Millinery...$4.89; Patent bluchers or tan calf button boots, $2.85; Heatherbloom and Molreen Petticoats, 99 cents; knitted vests, 75 cents; You'll want hosiery, 3 pairs for $1.00."

"What kind of hosiery?" Agnes asked.

"100 dozen of Ladies Cashmere Hose, fall or winter weight, with spliced ankles and heels, ribbed or plain...3 pairs for $1.00."

"We could each do with a pair. No corsets?"

"No, but there is a picture here of a 'Spirella' corset by

Ida E. Secord, Room 4, Smith Block, Rose Street. *'A style for every type of figure. The new long hipless front and back laced corset, pliable and hygenic, guaranteed not to break or rust.'* No price."

"Let me see." Agnes reached over for the paper. She was wearing rimless glasses with gold wire around her ears. She looked at the lacy image. Far too fancy. But perhaps Mrs. Ida Secord would copy her own comfortable corset, which had worn thin. The stays were cutting into her flesh.

A child from school came to ask Jessie to skip rope. Since it was Saturday morning, Agnes let Jessie go. She chanted with the children's voices outside

There is a maid lives on a mountain
Who she is I do not know
All she wants is gold and silver....

The whirr and clack of the treadle machine drowned out the rest. Agnes began to worry about the child's monthlies starting, and her unprepared. She should talk to her, but Agnes's mother never did. How did she learn? And did she want to be like her mother? No, Agnes Driver Mitton had been a remote uncaring parent who whacked her children so hard that her rings bit into their flesh.

It was Agnes's father, Robert, who had given her warmth and support, who had pointed out to her that puppies were the result of the dogs they saw mating on the streets. But had he told her about her monthlies?

After two years in Dame School she had had to work in the house, looking after her younger brothers and sisters. When Robert Mitton opened a second store, he took her into the new fruiterer's shop and taught her the business. She was quick, had a good business sense. He left his two sons,

Lennie and Bob, in the established greengrocery, which he had inherited from his father-in-law. He moved from one to the other. They were only a five minute walk apart in the Wilmslow Road. But at the end of the day, he was with Agnes to close up the shop and he walked her home. Then he talked, sometimes in adages, "Keep thy shop and thy shop will keep thee," and "Be not penny wise and pound foolish," but he also talked of family.

She loved the way her father cared about his father, Daniel, who lived with them. Daniel was a retired cavalry captain, on half pay in the reserves. He was the son, he said, of the richest man in England, John Mytton of Halston Hall, Shropshire. But John Mytton, being of unsound mind, had spent and given away his inheritance until there was nothing left. He was sent to Newgate prison for his debts, where he died. All Daniel had learned at Halston Hall was to shoot and ride a horse. So he failed into the army, hating the life, but having no other. He married down into trade in Withington. Not a happy marriage, but a necessary one, he having no fortune to recommend him to gentry. His son Robert had done the same. His father having no money, he worked for his father-in-law delivering fresh vegetables, before and after his marriage to the unlovable Agnes Driver. It was the way things were, Robert told her.

"You see, my lass, three generations from shirt sleeves to shirt sleeves."

"But did great-grandfather Mytton work in his shirt sleeves?"

Robert Mitton laughed. "No, no, much further back than that. We're yeoman stock come over with the Conqueror. *Mouton* was our name. Probably sheep herders in Normandy. But those who survived the fighting here were given houses and land so they could rule the English.

Now we are the English. Then my great-grandfather and his father had married land – particularly in Wales. They added to their estates by marrying plain women who inherited property."

"Poor women. To be married for your property."

"We all have a price on our heads, lass."

Agnes never did face that in marrying her Edward had "married down into trade" from generations of a Westmoreland parson's family; that his background made him insufferable, made him feel superior to ordinary work. He had had an inheritance – was that from Mary, his first wife? He had invested it in a woollen mill, had not insured the mill, which went up in flames. But that was before he began shopping at the Robert Mitton shops, a lonely widower. Robert promoted the match. After all, Agnes was single at twenty-six and drawn to the Primitive Methodists and temperance. Edward dressed and acted like a gentleman. A man in trade didn't ask a gentleman how he was going to support his daughter. Edward didn't. He had to move into the shops, which he took over when Robert died. He gambled them away.

CHAPTER 14

July 28, 1913

Jessie's new friend, Kitty Taylor, although always well-dressed, was a plump, hungry child. She loved to stay for a meal, and when asked, would phone her mother, who always said yes.

"Can Jessie and me go to the Exhibition on Opening Day, Mrs. Jackson?" she asked.

Agnes thought. She would have her sister, Fannie, staying with her, and she had to be on duty at the Women's Christian Temperance table for three hours. And the girls would hurry her through the exhibits. "I'll pack a lunch for you and keep it under the WCTU table," she said. "If I see you misbehaving, it's home with you, mind."

Jessie was thrilled. It was her first outing without family supervision. Her mother had given her fifty cents to spend. Everything cost five cents. She and Kitty went on the roundabout and the ferris wheel, screaming at the height. They ate a cob of buttered corn, and later pink candy floss which they licked while watching horse-pulling competitions, cheering the Belgians against the Percherons. They watched the Indians in pony races, in archery competitions, and in a tom-tom dance.

Fannie and George had come down from the farm to show their turkeys. George slept with his noisy turkeys out on the prairie in his new covered wagon, but he ate at 2929. At table George would explain to the others about farming, "Good crops, no market. No crops, good market." Besides turkeys and chickens and a cow on his half section, he now had wheat planted.

"Boom or bust, boom or bust, that's the nature of capitalism, Mr. Couling," Charles said. The adults at the table stiffened. This sounded like socialism. They all voted for, trusted in, the Conservative Party. Agnes changed the conversation.

Fannie slept with Agnes, who had arranged for Fannie to get dentures while in Regina. They were to be Agnes's gift to her sister, along with a dress.

When Agnes was off duty from the WCTU table, she found Fannie. They hurried past the livestock and grain entries to the garden vegetables, the flowers, the baking and preserving competitions. There was a table given to bachelors – there were so many of them on the farms as well as in the city. Farm boys had submitted homemade bread and butter and darned socks. Agnes was moved. Men were so weak compared to women, she was pleased to see them fending for themselves. And she was glad she had Fannie to share her enjoyment with. Fannie engaged the young men in conversation, unselfconscious of her toothless mouth, except for the two canines. They moved on to the sewing and knitting and crocheting. Agnes made mental notes of how she could expand and better her handwork. She must crochet antimacassars for the living room furniture. That Louis Rhys now slicked his hair back with brilliantine, the way Jack Foxxe did.

The two sisters chatted with the women behind the

counters. Then they sat at the Methodist Ladies' table and had tea and homemade scones with butter and jam.

When Agnes got back to the WCTU table, Jessie and Kitty were there, Jessie whining. They had eaten the egg sandwiches and drunk the lemonade Agnes had made them. But Jessie was out of money. Fifty cents was not enough. Agnes dug in her purse and produced another twenty-five cents. "Now that's it, Madam."

Jessie and Kitty ran off to the midway to play shooting games. When she was off duty again, Agnes went looking for the girls. On the midway she was appalled by the hawkers, the gambling, the drunkenness. The police were there, but they seemed to be turning a blind eye to the evil. Agnes found the girls at a shooting gallery and took them to look for Fannie. Jessie clutched a kewpie doll she had won.

The sun was in its western drop when they met Deborah and Miriam coming into the gate to the Exhibition. They were wearing pantaloons, an outrageous fashion that had been written up in the English newspapers as well as the local one. The girls were in high spirits. They were setting a fashion in Regina. Agnes was ashamed.

"Go home and take those trousers off," she muttered. "You look like women of ill repute. Are you going to perform in there?"

The girls laughed. "Don't be so conventional, Mother. This is the latest fashion. Why shouldn't we wear trousers? Men do. Besides, we're meeting Jack. He's parking his new Model T."

Fanny fingered the fabric of Miriam's pantaloons. "It feels like a bargain. Was it?"

Miriam stepped away. "Oh no, Auntie Fannie. How could you say that?"

"Conventionality is the wisdom of the ages," Agnes said quietly. "And you're gentlewomen, not street women. Now go home and change into proper clothing." Agnes was polite to Jack when he came to her house, but she did not like him. He lacked substance. She wished Miriam would go out with someone like Charles.

But Deborah and Miriam were swept inside with the crowds, and Agnes realized she had lost control of them. They were both earning good money. If she made too much of a fuss, they could leave. Then where would she be? Fannie took her arm as they crossed Railroad Street.

"Mothers and daughters disappoint each other," Fannie said.

Agnes's anger flamed. What did Fannie know about mothers and daughters when she had borne no children? "No, what happens to one, happens to the other," she countered. In their family they couldn't talk about what was important to them. They felt more comfortable talking in saws. But as they walked behind Jessie and Kitty, Agnes realized that her answer was not necessarily true. What happened to her daughters happened to her. But what happened to her – would it affect her daughters, or would they be so busy living their own lives that she would become unreal to them?

CHAPTER 15

September, 1913

Now that Edward Jackson was out of the house, Charles liked to read in "his" overstuffed chair which had a good reading lamp beside it. The other young people tended to go out in the evenings to choir practice, football, and concerts. Apart from participating in the monthly meetings of the Regina Debating Club, Charles would, after dinner, read newspapers, then books that analysed history. He had gone to a lecture by J.S. Woodsworth, a Methodist minister, who had challenged traditional views of history, had called the business and professional elite who frequented the Assiniboia Club "the smart set." Charles realized that his father, who was a minister in Kingston, Ontario, belonged to that "smart set," and that was his mother's life. She had tried to make Charles part of it, but he hated the dressing correctly, the teas, the card playing. He wanted his life to have the significance that J.S. Woodsworth suggested it could have.

He looked in the dining room, where Agnes and Jessie sat writing at the cleared table. They were sharing a bottle of Waterman's ink which sat between them on the wax-polished wood surface. Jessie was doing her homework and Agnes was writing her daily letter. She wrote with a good hand. Agnes had always written weekly to each of her sisters and brothers. Now she wrote weekly to Edward as well. She seemed not to get a reply from Edward, but she wrote consistently. It must be like writing into a vacuum, Charles decided.

Agnes's contradictions interested Charles. In England she had belonged to the Primitive Methodist church, a nonconformist return to the 18th century evangelical Methodism of John Wesley. Downright Dissenters, Mrs. Gaitskill would call them. They were a reactionary movement to the hierarchy that had crept into the church, and the building of buildings rather than person-to-person Christianity. Yet Agnes was an ardent royalist and she voted Conservative. She became as upset when a member of the royal family died as when her brother Bob died.

A few months previous Jessie had been reciting to Agnes the kings and queens of England, and the dates of battles they had fought. Agnes, who was sitting in the rocking chair darning the men's socks on a wooden egg, was able to correct Jessie in her recital. Charles had walked into the dining room. "This is all wrong, surely. Jessie should be learning Canadian history."

Agnes stiffened. She stopped darning. "There isn't any. Besides, this is what the school requires of her."

Don't interfere was the message Charles got. He went back to the chair in the living room, embarrassed. Agnes was right. The Canadian schools did teach English history. But living in the Niagara Peninsula, he had also been taught about United Empire loyalists – he was descended from them through his mother – and the battle of the Plains of Abraham. But that was from the English point of view. Canada was a colony. Was anyone writing Canadian history? He would go to the library and try to interest the child now that she was a Canadian.

Tonight Jessie called to Charles. "Come and hear my essay, Uncle Charles."

"Don't disturb your uncle when he's reading," Agnes said.

Charles came and sat on a dining chair next to Jessie.

"*No notable features recommended Regina as the site for urban settlement,*" Jessie read.

"*There was no water, poor drainage, no sheltering hills or timber for fuel, lumber or shade, but it had the heavy, stone-free soil necessary for wheat growing.*

"*For centuries other men had roamed this treeless, riverless land. They were migratory followers of the buffalo, who fed on the nutritious grasses that grew in clumps.*"

Jessie stumbled so over the words *migratory* and *nutritious* that Charles realized the child was copying her essay out of a library book. Agnes seemed not to recognize that this was plagiarism. She was counting on this child to graduate.

"Mam, the book says the Indians believed that the buffalo would return to the home of their ancestors when they were killed. Is that what will happen to us? We will go back to Manchester?"

"Stop talking nonsense and get on with your reading."

"*The Indians trapped the buffalo in pounds made from bush on the steep banks of Wascana Creek where the creek is high and wooded. The buffalo were chased into the pounds and down the steep banks of the creek, where they often broke their legs. Indians hiding in the bush killed the buffalo with bows and arrows.*"

That paragraph was better, Charles decided. It sounded more like a child's voice.

"The Indians made the buffalo meat into pemmican to feed them for the winter, and tanned the hides for clothing and blankets. The bones were left to bleach in the sun. When the white man came with the railroad, they called Regina Pile O' Bones."

Jessie stood up, flounced into the living room and did a pirouette in the centre of the Axmister carpet.

"Here, Miss, you put the lid on the ink bottle before it gets spilled," Agnes called.

"Are you finished your essay?" Charles asked.

Jessie nodded and went back to cover the ink bottle and put her work in her school bag.

"I read somewhere that the bones filled two acres as high as this house, and that it was the Crees who called this place Pile of Bones," Charles said. "And the Cree word for Pile of Bones is something like Wascana."

Jessie sat to listen.

"And that this place was called Wascana until the powers that be got the capital moved from Battleford to here, where they had bought lots of land and stood to profit. Then Princess Louise, the Governor General's lady, named it Regina after her mother Queen Victoria."

"She was right," Agnes said. "We are part of the British Empire still."

"I like Wascana better," Jesssie said.

"So do I." Charles said.

CHAPTER 16

January 1, 1914

In 1913 the Christmas and New Year's Eve rituals were carried out as usual, partly, Agnes felt, for Jessie and Billy who were still young. But Agnes had no stomach for it. She said, after they had sung *"Auld Lang Syne"* with locked arms in a circle, "Well, I'm glad that year is over."

In the kitchen, as she set the bread to rise over night, she thought about her brother Bob, who would never sing in a family circle again. He was such an agreeable boy, like Billy, in a way. Willing to please. And then to die like that. She wiped tears from her cheeks with her arm.

Up in her bedroom, after she had knelt to say her prayers and climbed into her lonely bed, her feet throbbed. She got up and put bed socks on. A phrase of *"The Holly and the Ivy"* surfaced – *"Oh, the holly bears a prickle, as sharp as any thorn..."* Agnes realized that despite the happiness she added to and took part in, she carried the painful thorn of Edward. In his silent way he had enjoyed Christmas season, family meals. He had been the one to say grace at table – "For what we are about to receive may the Lord make us truly thankful, Amen." That had established him as head of the table. Arnold would not take over, so Charles had. "Lord bless this food to our use, and our lives in thy service." Was that a better grace to say? Yes, probably. Edward was a traditionalist. Charles thought about everything he said and did.

Agnes wondered, as she wondered every night, how Edward was surviving in North Battleford. Of course he would be in a hospital building with central heating, but probably sharing with strangers, which he would hate. She feared he would have withdrawn further into his silent world. What was in that world?

Yet mail came from his family in England. She had forwarded those letters on to him. He had never shared his family with her since their marriage. She felt not good enough.

She wrote to Edward weekly, sent him a Christmas parcel, and small treats from time to time. But no word back. Well, she must wait and see.

CHAPTER 17

May 8, 1914

Deborah complained of the number of new dresses Agnes made for Miriam. Jack was taking Miriam to a dance a month and to concerts and to plays.

"Well, it's a poor house that can't afford one lady," Agnes said. "Besides, Miriam brings home the material and the patterns and does the machining. All I have to do is the handwork."

Deborah's romance with Louis was cooling. Although she was the right size, which was important to Louis, he found that Deborah – stood too close. Yes, that was it. She thrust her face close to his when she talked to him. He felt – clutched by her eyes, which were insistent. And her questions were insistent. He felt invaded. He retreated to the Regina Men's Choir and to rugby games to re-assert himself as a bachelor. Deborah retreated into reading *Anne of Green Gables*, and going to Mary Pickford moving pictures if Miriam were free. If not, her mother would go with her.

Dinner table talk began with the sinking of the Canadian Pacific liner, Empress of Ireland, in the Gulf of St. Lawrence, with one thousand lives aboard, and led to a heated discussion about the Komagata Maru, with over three hundred East Indians aboard, being chased out of Vancouver harbour without food or water by HMCS Rainbow. Charles was incensed that coloured immigrants would not be treated as well as British immigrants.

"They cause unemployment," Louis argued.

"How can they do that? They take on unskilled jobs that Brits won't touch."

Arnold winced. *No Englishmen need apply.* The signs were fewer, but obviously the British did not have a good reputation as workers, and certainly not as farmers.

"They lower wages for all of us by working for less."

"Then form labour unions and include them." A red flush was creeping up from Charles's collar.

A jaunty knock on the door ended the argument. Jack had arrived to take Miriam to the Northwest Mounted Police barracks for a ball. Louis used the interruption to escape to a rugby game. He found Charles heavy weather when he got into his debating mode.

Jack and Miriam had been to the barracks before – the Mounties often invited society to parties, and they were invited in turn. But this particular evening there had been a surprise snowfall. Jack wrapped Miriam in a buffalo robe in the open car. He was wearing the red uniform of an officer in the militia. His father had arranged the commission for him after he had spent two weeks at the militia summer training camp.

During the evening when Jack went outside to rev up his car so that it wouldn't freeze, Miriam was asked to dance by a tall policeman who had been watching her. He was a wonderful dancer, but he didn't talk.

Over supper Miriam asked another policeman who he was.

"Oh, that's Sergeant Richards, poor devil."

"Why poor devil?"

"Oh, his wife's got consumption. Not expected to live."

Miriam recognized Tom Richards as the policeman who had come to the house to check on Charles during the cyclone.

When Jack went out to rev his car again, Miriam walked over to Tom Richards and asked him to dance.

When the orchestra played *"If you were the only girl in the world,"* Jack swept her onto the floor. He kissed her neck. "This is our song," he said, singing fragments of it. "Remember that. This is our song."

Driving home, Jack became ardent. Miriam laughed at him. But when he parked outside 2929 he took her hand and said, "Look, I'm crazy about you. I can't get you off my mind. I can't sleep nights for thinking about you."

"Don't be so silly," Miriam said.

"No, Miriam, you must be serious. You've given me a purpose in life, a future. You're my future. And if this war in Europe develops, I will have to go. I need you to come home to."

Miriam was impressed. Someone wanted her, needed her, to be his future. She let him kiss her. She liked being loved.

CHAPTER 18

August 4, 1914

The hardware store closed half an hour early so that the staff could join the crowd that was roaring outside The Leader office. A large sign had been posted: **WAR!** A small group began singing *"God Save the King"* and *"The Maple Leaf."* Hats were taken off, then thrown in the air. Flags were waved. A mountie, a city policeman, a Danish-Canadian, a Serbian-Canadian made impromptu speeches that no one could hear. Arnold was outraged when he heard the policeman's southern English accent. *So why did you emigrate if England is so great? Go back and be jobless there!* he wanted to shout back at the man. Firecrackers exploded. A car carrying on its hood a bulldog draped in the Union Jack forced its way through the crowds. Militia men, already in hot serge khaki uniforms, stood at the edge of the crowd. When *"God Save the King"* broke out again, Arnold did not take off his hat. It was knocked off his head. He turned in anger, his fists ready. A woman in a broad-brimmed hat had lifted Arnold's fedora with her parasol. Arnold scowled at her, recovered his hat and left. A Boy Scout band marched towards him playing *"Land of Hope and Glory."* A recruiting officer sat at a table signing up a long line of unemployed.

Arnold managed to buy a paper and walked home reading it. Canada had offered Britain an infantry division. That was a lot of men. Reservists in the British and Serbian armies were leaving to join their regiments. The Canadian militia was called up to drill and be on twenty-four hour patrol. He wondered if Jack would have to go. Jack had urged Arnold to join the militia with him, but Arnold had laughed at him, protesting that he was not a military man.

His mother was lying on the chesterfield, her back to the world. When he was a child she had become upset daily about the casualty lists in the Boer War. Then when the blind and maimed ex-soldiers appeared on the streets selling boot-laces and matches, she recoiled in horror that men would do this to each other. She was upset now. What good did it do?

"A recruiting table has been set up in our school," Jessie announced to the dinner table.

"They surely aren't recruiting school boys," Agnes said, passing potatoes and peas fresh from the garden. The vegetables smelled of the fresh mint she had put in the cooking water.

"They'll recruit them as cadets, send them to summer camp, then when they are eighteen, over they go," Charles said dryly.

The cruel meaning of war is lost on the young. They have no memories, Agnes thought.

"It will all be over by Christmas. What has Serbia to do with us?" Arnold said.

"I fervently hope so, but it may not be," Charles said.

"The question now, Buster, is what has Belgium to do with us?" Louis said. "Who's doing the recruiting?"

"Feel the tug of war?" Arnold smiled.

"Well, I might get a free trip back to see my father

and my sister," Louis said.

"You might get a free trip back to them in a box," Charles said.

Billy watched the faces of the men as he ate.

"To answer your question, old man," Arnold said, pulling a newspaper out of his pocket, "J.F.L. Embury has been given command of the 95th Regiment. He is to recruit a unit for overseas – the 28th Battalion, Canadian Expeditionary Force. There will be two reserve battalions, the 68th and the 195th."

"I'm amazed," Louis said. "I thought we'd be attached as skivvies to some elite Toronto regiment."

That evening the four young men sat around the living room after the others had gone to bed. Billy, seated on a footstool beside the fireplace, put down the comics he had been reading and began shaving with his penknife a thick cake of tobacco. He packed the shavings into a pipe he had just bought himself. When he lit it and drew on it, he coughed. He persisted. When the pipe warmed up, it hurt his split lip. Arnold shook his head at him. Billy tapped the pipe out into the fireplace. Arnold passed him a cigarette.

"What are you going to do?" Louis asked Arnold, lighting Billy's cigarette.

"Do? I'm going to do nothing. I'm a Canadian now. It isn't Canada's concern that Germany invades Belgium."

"Canada is part of the British Empire," Charles said.

"It's my concern," Louis said. "My mother was Belgian. I've been to Liege to visit my grandmother and aunts. I worry about them with this Hun invasion."

"How did you manage to get a Belgian mother?" Arnold asked.

"My grandparents were Catholics," Louis said. "There

was no good Catholic school in Cardiff, so my father was sent to a Belgian school. That's where he met my mother, who was brave enough to move to Wales when she married. We spoke French at home."

"Do you speak Welsh?" Charles asked.

Louis replied. *"Rydw i'n dyfgu Cymraig."*

"And French?"

Louis replied *"D'accord. On parlait français chez nous."*

"What happened to the Catholicism?"

"Oh, my mother died when my sister was born, and after that, my father didn't care much what my sister and I did. We began going to school with the other kids in our street. Our housekeeper could speak only Welsh. She took me to chapel, where I learned to sing."

"I envy you that," Charles said.

"The singing? But not losing my mother at the age of five. She was a saint. My world has never been the same."

"So what are you going to do about it?" Arnold asked.

"At the moment, nothing. With the line-ups of unemployed, they don't need men who are holding down a job. And I couldn't live on seventy-five cents a day. Let's hope it may all blow over."

"I heard at work that Garnet Durham has accepted only 170 of 600 applicants."

"Poor devils. Not even seventy-five cents a day," Charles said.

"Look, Charles, what do you want from life? What's important?" Louis asked.

"Marriage, children, a job I find interesting."

Louis's eyes filled and he smiled.

"That's crazy," Arnold said, leaning towards Charles, who now always sat in Edward's chair. "Marriage is just a battleground. Children are just mouths to feed, little responsibilities. And who knows how they will grow up?"

"It's one of the chances you take. But I think that's what life's about."

"Charles is right," Louis said. "That's what life's about. Also, face it, sex is a necessity. I think about women's bodies all the time, don't you? I want to undress them all."

Charles smiled agreement, then glancing at Billy, said, "If you want lots of sexual partners, you're in for a lot of pleasure, but you won't have a family. What about you, Arnold?"

"Not for me," Arnold said. "Oh, I may have bizarre dreams, but when I'm awake I'm dreaming of working for myself building houses, travelling, moving out to the Coast, away from this hostile climate. I've had enough of women growing up in this family."

Louis turned to Charles. "But you want to get married, once your sister is provided for, don't you?"

"My sister?" Charles exclaimed. "It wouldn't occur to me to provide for her. She has a good job with the government. Why should I look after her?"

Louis seemed subdued.

"So you have to provide for your sister back in Wales?" Charles asked.

"I send money every month," Louis said. "Which makes it hard to get ahead. If you're middle class in Britain, girls are not expected to go out in the world and work."

"I've had a narrow escape with three of them," Arnold said.

"But you do plan to marry," Charles asked Louis.

"Let's say I hope to," Louis said, "when I meet the right girl."

The others heard him and realized his attachment to Deborah was over.

"You wouldn't seriously think of joining up, would you?" Arnold asked.

"Well, I have a loyalty to Belgium. To hear of her being invaded makes me want to fight the bullies."

"Don't give it a thought. You'd fail the marksmanship test anyway," Arnold laughed. Louis seldom brought home a bird when they went out shooting.

"Well, let's talk about pleasanter things," Louis said. "What about you, Charles? So you plan to marry?"

"Yes, I'm looking for a woman to share my life with. Someone to come home to."

The other men heard him. Yes, Charles was the closest to being able to marry. His job paid well, he'd had a promotion, and his father being a minister, the family were comfortably off.

Arnold leaned back on the chesterfield and was silent. Was sex a necessity to him? He was exhausted by the end of most days, so he didn't give it much thought until the weekend. Then he would rather be out on the prairie shooting, or playing soccer or hockey with the men. Yes, that's what he enjoyed, the company of men. And as for a job – he hoped to move into farm machinery with Massey Harris or International Harvester. He had already put his applications in with those firms. But to be married to a girl like his sisters – it was unthinkable. Even Miriam was becoming silly and fractious. And she was spending too much time with Jack Foxxe. He was a bad influence on her, wanting to dance all the time and skate and go to the theatre. If he took advantage of Miriam's innocence Arnold would smash his pretty face in.

"What's important to you, Buster? how do you want to spend your life?"

"Getting through the next day," Arnold answered.

CHAPTER 19

August, 1914

Whenar became inevitable, Jack was elated. He would be among the first to go, which meant he would be in the thick of things. He would cross the Atlantic with his unit, the 5th Western Cavalry, then he would transfer to the Royal Flying Corps. He wanted to learn to fly.

"It's my chance to test myself, to prove myself," he said to Miriam when she cried. He was pleased that she cried.

He bought Miriam a diamond ring with their names inscribed inside the band, and gave it to her out on the prairie as they watched the huge pink-gold sun slide under the horizon. Over dinner at 2929 they showed the ring to the family. Only Deborah and Jessie showed surface enthusiasm. Finally Agnes said, "You must forgive us. We're worried about the war, and your having to go."

"But it may be over before I see any action," Jack complained. He offered to sell his Model T car to the men present, but no one wanted it. They could walk to work from 2929, and the prospect of making trips on prairie roads, changing flat tires, did not appeal to them.

When he had driven off with Miriam, Agnes said,

"Well, he's a pretty man."

Arnold laughed. "Is that all you can say?"

"Well, you're the one who knows him. What can you add?"

"Nothing," Arnold said, his face grim. He picked up a newspaper to end the conversation.

The men sat around the table smoking while the women cleared up the kitchen and washed the dishes.

"He seems unformed, youthful," Charles said. "I'm sure Miriam will make a man of him over time. I rather envy him his exuberance."

Louis picked up a piece of the newspaper, then peeked from behind it. "He seems quick to want to sell us his car."

"He'll sell you anything if it brings a profit," Arnold said.

"When all other sins are old, avarice is still young," Louis quoted.

"Where did you hear that?" Arnold asked.

"My Belgian grandmother."

"That's a harsh thing to say of your new brother-in-law-elect," Charles said to Arnold.

"He's not who I would choose for Miriam," Arnold said. "You should hear his advice on how to get ahead. Not only do you join a church for contacts, but clubs, and recently he has advised me to join, to contribute to, not one, but both political parties, so that you can lean on whoever is elected for favors."

"That's appalling."

"In what way?"

"It's so damaging to your integrity as a human being."

Billy's glance went from face to face. Louis noticed he was out of his depth. Louis too was out of his depth. "What the hell do you mean by that?" he asked Charles.

"Sometimes you talk such rot." He blew smoke at Charles who didn't smoke.

Charles was flustered. He hated being challenged. "I mean..." he said slowly, "that you have to like the person you see in the mirror every day when you are shaving."

"How d'you come to like who you see in the mirror, Charlie?" Arnold asked. "Most of us don't."

Charles sighed and looked at the blue and white plates he loved on the plate rack opposite him. How could he explain integrity? "I suppose you behave in a way that seems decent and trustworthy, that people matter more to you than making money or getting ahead."

Arnold smiled to himself. People were not important to him. Mostly they made him miserable.

Billy pulled on his chin to reveal his tongue circling his mouth. He stared at Charles.

"Jack would like his image in the mirror," Louis said. "As Mrs. Jackson said, he's a pretty man."

"I'm not talking about appearances. I'm talking about the inner core, the decisions you make every day that form you."

"Like what?"

"Like treating people with the same respect, dignity, that you expect from them. Like not making use of other people."

"That's it, that's him!" Arnold said, slamming his fist on the table. "And by God, if I find that he's making use of Miriam, I'll kill him!"

The others laughed at him, and Arnold was pleased. He loved the company of men. He loved their talk. And Charles had put into words what he had been feeling when he was with Jack.

"He has no inner core, that's the problem with him,"

Arnold went on.

"Well, he's young yet and unformed. He may have terrible parents," Charles said.

"We all have...parents," Arnold said. "That's no excuse for being like them."

Louis and Billy glanced at the kitchen door and Louis stood up. "Come on, Billy. I'll treat you to the Red and Blacks game," he said.

CHAPTER 20

August, 1914

Jack told Miriam that she was invited to dinner with his parents. Neither of them wanted to go. "But you're going to have to join that family too, and they will become grandparents to our children," Jack laughed.

Miriam hadn't thought ahead to children, but she did want her own house to fix up. When she stepped inside the Foxxe house down by Wascana lake she gasped. She was used to new houses – Regina was a new city – but all the furnishings in the Foxxe house were new. Miriam worked in the office of the R.H. Williams Department Store. In her lunch break she wandered in the various departments, and knew the stock. Moreover Mirabelle Foxxe, Jack's mother, was wearing a new cream and brown crêpe dress, the latest fashion in the store.

Mirabelle Foxxe was a pretty woman, even taller than Miriam. She carried her head high, and had her dark hair coiled into a chignon. Despite her carriage, she seemed nervous. Mr. Foxxe had been delayed at work, would Miriam like to see the house? Miriam trailed after her, making polite noises, but wondering why the house, room after room, felt so empty. And there was no smell of dinner cooking.

"Would you like sherry while we wait?" Mirabelle asked. "Jack dear, ask the maid to bring in the tray of drinks, please."

The maid, in a tight black and white uniform, turned out to be Julia, Agnes's Romanian cleaning help. Julia grinned when she recognized Miriam. She was wearing just one petticoat by the shape of her.

"You know the maid?" Mirabelle asked as Jack poured sherry.

"Oh yes, Julia. She comes to help my mother two days a week. Usually with more petticoats."

Mirabelle smiled. They had made a connection. "I had to persuade her to take several off to squeeze into the uniform," she said.

Jack's father burst into the room, came over to Miriam and pumped her hand. "So this is the incomparable Miriam," he said. "What a beauty you are. No wonder Jack didn't want you to get away." He was a stocky, florid man with a circle of greying hair.

"I hope he loves me for more than my looks," Miriam said. "They will change."

"Never!" Jack and his father said together.

At the dinner table Mirabelle asked, "What does your father do, Miriam?"

Miriam's eyes stung. She reached for her glass of water.

"He's a builder like father," Jack answered. "But Mr. Jackson is retired."

"I must meet him," John Foxxe said. "We have much in common."

"Not just now, you won't," Jack said. "Mr. Jackson is a restless traveller. No sooner does he come home than he's off somewhere else."

"Does your mother not travel with him?" Mirabelle asked.

"No, my mother suffers from travel sickness," Miriam said. She was beginning to appreciate Jack's way of handling inappropriate questions.

"Mother, is there any gravy for these cutlets? They're very dry."

"No, I don't think the maid cooked gravy," Mirabelle said.

Miriam could see why Jack preferred to eat at 2929. The potatoes were dry, the peas and carrots were canned. The bread, and the raisin pie for dessert, had come from a bakery. Much was left uneaten. She smiled inwardly hearing her mother pronounce, "Why, we could live on what they waste." Would the two families ever meet?

"What are you feeling?" Jack asked Miriam as he drove her home.

"Sad," Miriam said.

"Sad that I'm going away? But I'll be back before you know it and then we'll get married."

Will we? Miriam wondered. "No, for some reason that house makes me feel sad. It seems so...empty. Jack, I don't want to live like that."

"You won't. We won't. You see, Miriam, you've got to understand my mother. She grew up poor in St. Louis and went on the stage. That's where my parents met. My father was off a farm in Kentucky, but he had gone into building. I suppose he was a carpenter in the early days. He moved from St. Louis to Toronto to here, wherever building was going on. He had no money, so he would build a house, live in it, sell it for a hefty profit, and build a bigger one. My poor mother has had to move to a new house every year or two. Even here, where he has prospered enough to buy land

and be elected to council, he keeps seeing a better location opening up for them to live in. So she has to move again. And he makes her join the Assiniboine Club, and the IODE and the Musical Society for contacts. I sometimes feel she is acting a role, even the role of mother. I feel so sorry for her, but he is a force of nature, and she has no money of her own."

Miriam leaned over and kissed Jack. She not only loved him, she now liked him.

CHAPTER 21

August, 1914

Miriam had been proud of Jack when he paraded on a horse in his red militia officer's uniform. Now that he was going off to war, his uniform was tight khaki, his hat a visored one. He still looked handsome, sitting erect on his horse, looking straight forward, as the 5th Western Cavalry under Captain George Tuxford paraded to the station to board the train for Montreal. Miriam did not go to the station. She and Jack had stayed up making love and vows all the night before. Miriam could not deal with Jack's parents. They might disapprove of her behaviour, as her mother did. She didn't care, compared to their great love, but she did care.

But Agnes, Deborah and Jessie followed the crowds to the station. Patriotism coursed through Agnes, making her feel vital, part of an Empire that was vast and important. When the anthem *"Land of Hope and Glory"* broke out, Agnes sang aloud, tears sliding down her cheeks.

When Jack spotted Agnes and the girls he had his parents fight through the crowd to meet them. John Foxxe put out his hand and gave each a hearty shake, saying to Agnes he could see where Miriam got her beauty. Jack's mother seemed numb. She gave an inert gloved hand to each of them, but she could say nothing.

As Jack boarded the train, Agnes sang with the crowd, *"God go with you till we meet again."* When the train had pulled out, leaving only steam behind, Agnes turned to Jack's parents, but they were nowhere to be seen. She took both of her girls by the arm and hurried them home.

On the sidewalk outside 2929 were two guns and the bodies of six jackrabbits. Deborah and Jessie gasped in horror.

"What's this all about? Where are those men?" Agnes asked. Not getting an answer, she said, "Now, you lot, grab three rabbits each by the ears, and I'll take the guns. It's careless to leave them out in the street."

Jack had given Miriam his Model T to drive for the few weeks he would be at war. When Arnold came home with Louis and Billy from hunting on the prairie, he stopped and laughed at the car parked in front of 2929. "So the chickens have come home to roost," he said, putting his gun and catch down on the sidewalk.

"What d'you mean by that?" Louis demanded, examining the car.

"What goes around comes around," Arnold said, unwilling to tell Louis the history of the car.

Louis put his gun down and jumped into the driver's seat, saying, "Tell me what to do, Buster." Billy climbed in the passenger seat.

Arnold identified the three pedals on the floor, forward, reverse, and neutral, and the brake lever. "Let's see if it works," Arnold said. "Where's the crank?" Billy handed him the crank, which had been resting on the floor.

"Put your foot on the neutral pedal." Arnold turned on the gas feed lever on the steering wheel, and ran to the front of the car to crank it up. When the engine engaged, he ran back to adjust the gas lever. Louis depressed the forward pedal and the car shot off, Arnold on the running board clinging to the driver's door. He shouted to Louis to put the car in neutral, to put the brake on, but Louis was having too much fun. He and Billy whooped as they drove all over Regina, Louis squeezing the rubber bulb horn, which scared no one with its tooting. They ran out of gas on the Albert Street bridge. Louis persuaded Arnold to get a tin of gas from the hardware store – Arnold had a key. They found the gas tank under the front seat. Beside it was a ruler. The tank measured empty. Arnold poured a gallon of gas in, then had Louis do the cranking. The car did not like to start on so little gas, but when it engaged, Arnold shot off, leaving Louis to walk home, carrying the crank.

Over dinner Miriam seemed indifferent to the men's escapade with Jack's car. "When summer comes, we'll drive you to Regina Beach," Louis promised her, feeling guilty about driving off without her permission.

"Don't be silly, Louis. Jack will be back by then. He'll take me to Regina Beach." Billy made one of his rare ventures into language. "W'ere'ya going ta keep it over winter, Buster?" He said it quickly, hoping Agnes would not hear and correct his speech.

Arnold suppressed his immediate reaction, *Not my problem*, and glanced at Miriam. It was his problem. "I'll ask them at work if I can put it in the storage shed," he said. "There's lots of room."

Miriam became upset by the letters from Jack. He wrote to her as if she didn't exist, except in his memory. He didn't spare her when he wrote of the good time he was having, seeing the world, eating splendid meals, dancing with pretty nurses. He seemed to be having such a good time, and she was miserable in Regina without him. Why should she be the one to wear a diamond ring? Why couldn't he? She took the ring off and left it in a drawer one whole Sunday, but then she put it on again to go to work. People would ask questions.

CHAPTER 22

1914

"montreal dearest Miriam the train ride across canada was perfecto I have a servant to myself called a batman a poor farm boy called Jim from south of weyburn he knows nothing of how to care for my things except to carry my kit so I have to teach him everything even how to salute he will learn these things once we get to england I am learning which wines to drink with each course wouldnt our mothers be surprised the food is wonderful and I play cards with the other officers losing mostly but I am learning oh this is going to be great love from your Jack."

"plymouth england dearest Miriam the crossing was fine such good food and service and there were lots of nurses on board who only could dance with officers so I danced my way across the atlantic the men so boisterous they threw a provost sargent overboard there were sparks flying over that he

was saved but was in sick bay the whole trip then the men refused to unload their gear saying they came to fight germans not to be navvies so the poor british milisha no uniforms were sent to unload us Ive been given a weeks disembarkation leave and a railroad pass so will head for london your Jack"

"london dear Miriam I wish you were here I know no one I will bring you here one day the tiny trains travel so fast and without vibrashun women are driving the street cars and delivry waggons and taxi cabs in london and even smoking and drinking whiskey in public the food is awful how did your mother learn to be such a good cook I went to see a musical called chu chin chow it was very good back to salsbury tomorrow I miss you so your Jack"

"salsbury plains dear father can you get me out of here and into the RFC? it hasnt stopped raining since we got here and we are all in tents our clothes soaking wet all the time and the tight-fitting tunics splitting down the back and these cheap greatcoats don't keep out the rain the cold or the wind and these cheap boots are falling apart the men get just tea and porridge for breakfast stew for lunch and bread and tea and jam for dinner Im afraid they will mutinny not that our food is much better but at least it isnt ladled into a tin thank mother for the food parcel would she include some tins of meat in the next one and some sweet caps your son Jack" *"salsbury dear father the* RFC *didnt work out at least I was in warm barracks for a week but the officers were rude and called me a boy scout and said things like so he wants to learn to fly well we wont make it any easier than fighting in the trenches and they had me wait on table then said I had a poor attitude and woodnt let me in so I went back to my unit on salsbury they are now in unheated huts but my* CO *said there were too many officers in the canadian contingent and I would have to be an enlisted man can you get me my commishun back your son Jack"*

CHAPTER 23

September 6, 1914

Charles Wilson was in love with 2929 12th Avenue. The living room furniture was overstuffed dark green tapestry. Comfortable. The piano, a Heintzman, was oak. The pictures were reprints of 17th century Dutch interiors, framed in dark wood. The dining room was brighter. Mrs. Jackson kept the large oak table covered in the daytime with a dark green velour cover. For meals a snowy white damask cloth was thrown over a quilted cotton silence cloth, and linen napkins were rolled into silver plated napkin holders. The oak sideboard had a bevelled mirror inset. Charles liked to sit facing the plate rack high on the wall facing the window. There Mrs. Jackson displayed her best blue and white English china.

In the summer evenings he had taken over Edward's gardening chores, with Agnes showing him what she knew. The garden was his sanctuary. In the short summer months Charles gave up going to church, much as he loved the language of the Anglican service. He felt closer to God digging the black clay, planting and pulling and gathering and feeding the hens and geese than he did in a church building listening to sermons by a man...like his father who was...Charles faced it...not as bright as he. Yes, now that he accepted his father's limitations, he accepted him more, was able to write home. His mother he had more difficulty with. She was so caught up in the role of Minister's Wife that appearances dominated her. What would others think? Also, she needed to feel superior to others, often calling members of the congregation pathetic. Charles's childhood and that of his sister had seemed cramped, suffocating.

Louis had asked him, "What do you do for fun, Charlie?" For days afterwards Charles had asked himself that question. Fun? What was that? There were only duties and responsibilities in a minister's family. One had to be a model to the rest of the community of the Christian life. Thinking back on his childhood made him seethe with anger. The long summer evenings, after gardening, he would hike out on the prairie until he had walked the anger out of himself. He realized that skating and hockey were now fun for him, but he had learned them during his one year in college, away from home, when he had bought himself second-hand skates and a friend had held him up and coached him. He was so enchanted with the freedom of skating, the fun of hockey, that he had scraped through his first year academically. His parents said there wasn't the money for his kind of marks if he didn't win scholarships. He moved out west to seek his fortune.

Here at 2929, he enjoyed Mrs. Jackson's company when she would find time to chat about her family and her time in England. She was clever, could have run a large business if she were not a woman. Charles always volunteered to hold her hanks of wool on his spread arms while she rolled the yarn into balls. Then she would start talking, and would sit back and chat rather than finding something that must be done.

Deborah was still "moping," as her mother called it, for Louis, who had joined the Regina Men's Choir, and went constantly to rugby games as if he were a player. When he came home from games he was chewing gum. But that didn't fool the others. He had been drinking beer.

One evening when Louis was home he agreed to play the piano for a while. Deborah asked him to play *"Believe Me if all those Endearing Young Charms."* Louis said sorry, he couldn't remember that one. How about...and he played and sang, *"Pack Up Your Troubles."* Deborah looked devastated. Everyone was now singing war songs – *"It's a Long Way to Tipperary"* and *"Keep the Home Fires Burning."* Louis learned them as soon as he heard them.

The next day, after dinner, Charles asked Deborah to walk on the prairie, to see if they could hear the meadowlark sing and to look for wild flowers. He loved the way the horizon expanded when they walked away from the city. And there was always a wind whistling its unique tune, and the long grasses singing theirs.

"You know, that song, *'Believe Me if all those Endearing Young Charms,'* is lovely in its way, but the poet Yeats said it better," Charles said.

"Oh, do tell me," Deborah said.

Charles took her hand, and recited, as they walked south over the tough prairie grass towards Wascana Creek,

When you are old and grey and full of sleep
And nodding by the fire, take down this book
And slowly read, and dream of the soft look
Your eyes held once, and of their shadows deep

How many loved your moments of glad grace
And loved your beauty with love false or true
But one man loved the pilgrim soul in you
And loved the sorrows of your changing face

"Oh, to be so loved," said Deborah, stopping in front of Charles and looking up at him. Deborah tilted her head up, expecting to be kissed, as all heroines were in the romances she read. But Charles took her hand and walked on, trying to remember the third verse which Deborah had interrupted.

"He's not the least romantic," Deborah would tell Miriam.

To hide her disappointment, Deborah found a clump of bullrushes growing beside the creek. She demanded that Charles cut some for her to put in the umbrella stand in the front hall. Charles was going to draw Deborah's attention to the reflection of blue sky and massed white clouds in the water, when he slid in the wet mud. He clung to one bullrush as he struggled to cut the thick stocks of others with his pen knife. His shoes had filled with mud and water, but he didn't complain. As he handed the bullrushes to Deborah, he wanted to own her youthful spontaneity. And more, he loved the way she seemed to care for him. She had put the bullrushes down and held out her hands to pull him up the bank, laughing. He couldn't kiss her. The war was going badly for the Allies. If conscription passed parliament, he might be called up.

"Why did you come?" Deborah asked.

"Come?"

"From Ontario. I hear the Niagara Peninsula is lovely, with a much better climate."

Charles couldn't resist. "I came looking for you." He smiled down at her. "Actually, I came partly to seek my fortune in a new part of the country, and partly because I couldn't breathe in London, Ontario."

"You have asthma?"

Charles laughed. "No. You are a sweet lady, d'you know that?"

"Am I? So why couldn't you breathe in Ontario?"

"Everything is so regimented, done in a certain way. Now, it's strange for an accountant to object to that. And I do love the orderliness of my books. But Deborah, I want to change the world!" Colour came into his pale skin and his green eyes shone down on her.

Deborah was in love with someone who was going to change the world.

The prairie winds whistled around them as they turned towards home.

CHAPTER 24

1914 – 1915

"london dear father thank you for getting me this commishun in the PPCLI *I hope it didn't cost too much in ottawa Im sorry you had to mortgage the house I will pay you back when I get home but this is much better and we are on our way to france december 20th – oh Im not supposed to write that Id better scratch it out will you phone Miriam and tell her my news I havent had time to write its been such a scramble but I am really looking forward to seeing action in france your son Jack"*

"dearest Miriam what a wonderful Xmas parcel I got from you I needed the balaclava did you knit it and the sweet cap cigarettes the turkish delights lumped together why dont you make chocolate fudge instead and thank your mother for the Xmas cake and shortbread quite a surprise yesterday the brits started singing Xmas carols and the germans joined in yes we are that close to them

but they don't seem like enemy just men like us I love you and miss you your Jack"

"petrograd hotel london dear buster I am writing to you as I dont want to upset Miriam or my parents and yet I have to tell somebody the nightmare this is I have a few weeks off in blitie having a broken leg from a shell when we got ashore in france I was so excited – wine was 20 francs a bottle good food and lots of pretty women but the next day they moved us up to the front and at the railroad we saw the men coming down the line they looked like ghosts so pale even those who could walk and they didnt look at us or talk to us when I got to the front at Ypres I could see why the salient is one huge wet artillry target with the germans on the high ground we were replacing the french – apparently two of their units vamoosed when the gas came we fought for two weeks we were supposed to get the german trenches at polygon wood it was hell non-stop shelling on the last day the germans turned their full attention on us we had to put all the signallers cooks batmen and orderlies in the line and we held but buster we were surrounded by dead decaying bodies and we could do nothing for the screams and cries of the wounded only 4 of us officers got out and 150 of the men they left me six hours in the trench with the corpses and rats I was so afraid of getting infection in my wound and losing my leg it was like being kicked by a horse then the pain started but someone did come during the night and got me

out and now the pain has stopped and I am getting good care but the smell of death wakes me up
at night your friend Jack Foxxe PS they tell me we
held the line"

"dear buster – back to base camp with a limp the
majors and colonels living so well here sending us
young ones up the line to be killed a name on an
honour roll I hated going back to the front all
green men fresh from canada the others were
mostly brits but all casualties and how the men
hate us you want to do everything you can for the
men in your platoon but we have to see that they
obey the most awful orders that we do not want
to obey urging them over the top to certain death
but the price of mutiny is court martial the boche
must hate it as much as we do look after Miriam
for me I love her so your friend Jack Foxxe"

CHAPTER 25

Summer, 1915

O
n summer Sundays Billy got up early to go shooting with Arnold. In the afternoons he liked to go to South Railway Street to see if the soldiers were parading to the station. He often saw Miriam there. After Jack had been wounded at Second Ypres, she began a mournful haunting of the departing trains. But she didn't see Billy. She seemed not to see anyone.

As the soldiers paraded along the street, Billy laughed to see a golden retriever running alongside one platoon. When he got to the station platform he sought out the dog to pet it. The young owner of the dog said it's name was Roger and it was the platoon's mascot. But when the soldiers tried to hustle the dog aboard the train, a sergeant called, "Off with that dog!" The owner brought Roger off the train and handed his rope to Billy. "Keep him for me, kid. I'll get him when I come back." He gave Billy two dollars.

When Billy came up the front porch of 2929 with the dog, Arnold was sitting in what used to be his father's chair, reading the papers. Agnes, who seemed to know everything that was going on, met Billy at the door, her sleeves rolled up, her hands on her hips. "Well, what's this all about?"

Billy found his voice. "A sojer gave 'im to me to look after until he comes back."

"Soldier," Agnes pronounced the word carefully. "You have to curl your tongue when you're speaking, Billy. You can't let it sit in your mouth like a pancake. Well, take him around the back and tie him under the back stoop. No, those geese will worry the life out of him. Arnold, you solve this problem. You'll have to walk him, mind you, Billy boy."

The dog crouched, looking from new owner to new owner for acceptance.

"He looks like Billy," Miriam laughed in the kitchen after dinner.

Agnes was glad enough to have an animal to give the soup bones to. The fowl would have to share the table scraps.

CHAPTER 26

Summer, 1915

At first Agnes did not like Dr. Gaspard, who had written asking her to come to North Battleford Provincial Mental Hospital. He was sixtyish, his beard was unkempt, his brown suit was crumpled, and he lounged in his chair. But as he talked, Agnes detected a caring, a compassion for his patients, who were to Agnes, as she had walked through the grounds and the building, frighteningly unattractive.

"Your husband doesn't belong here, Mrs. Jackson," Dr. Gaspard said.

I could have told you that, Agnes said to herself.

"But the law has put him here, and we have done what we can to understand him, but he won't talk."

"He has never been one to talk," Agnes said.

"I see him as a deeply unhappy man."

"I think he has been unhappy all his life."

Dr. Gaspard managed a wry smile. "Yes, but we are not born unhappy. I doubt that as a small boy he was unhappy. It's how we react to life's blows that determines our fate."

What does he mean by that? Agnes wondered. *What is our fate?*

"I mean by fate one's personality, way of dealing with the rest of life. He seems in retreat, to live in his own imaginary world. Therefore I can't produce a diagnosis, even if we had the tools to acurately diagnose mental illnesses. It could be schizophrenia, it could be depression. Do you think his angry outburst was in reaction to a stressful situation, or was it out of the blue, entirely unexpected?"

"Oh, he is an angry man," Agnes said. "He is often angry."

"But also withdrawn?"

Agnes hadn't thought of Edward that way. She assumed when he didn't speak, he was angry.

"Tell me – and I should have asked for this information long ago – did he suffer losses as a child, as a young man? Parental losses? Siblings?"

"Oh yes. His mother died when he was young, and his first wife died in childbirth, and so did the child. And we lost a son to diphtheria."

"Oh." Dr. Gaspard got up, moved to the window. "I should have known this long ago." He stuffed a pipe and lit it, looking out the window. "You know, we are not given much information on patients who are committed at his majesty's pleasure. They see us as a kind of prison rather than a healing place.... You see, Mrs. Jackson, if we don't grieve enough at the time of a loss, the grief may come out throughout one's life as depression, anger. Would you say Mr. Jackson was depressed?"

"I couldn't say. Withdrawn, yes. He lived in his own world within our world. And..." Agnes hated to say it, "he was a gambler."

"That's an unrealistic view of life, certainly." Dr. Gaspard came back to his chair. "Has he ever cried?"

"The men in our family don't cry."

"The cruellest strictures to put on a small boy. Don't express your feelings. Be brave. Be a hero, not a human being. How are we going to help all these young men we have sent off to hell, saying be brave, be a hero, when they are feeling scared for their lives? Well, that's not your problem.... It was good of you to come all this way, Mrs. Jackson. It has helped me to understand your husband. Now, I suppose you would like to see him. I have arranged tea for you in a little private room at the end of the hall."

Edward was sitting reading a newspaper when Agnes came in. He looked ravaged, and was wearing glasses with steel rims. When he saw Agnes his mouth flickered a smile, his eyes devoured her. He stood up, and Agnes embraced him. He was skin and bones. He wasn't eating. He did not want to let her go.

When she sat to pour tea for him, to put butter and jam on his scones as she had always done, she told of the slow train trip to Saskatoon and then to North Battleford. She glanced at him. He wasn't listening. She told him about each of the family members. He wasn't listening. She told him of his garden and his geese. He was listening. That was his world.

Agnes could not stay in a hotel. She never had and never would. She had planned to take the evening train back, arriving in the middle of the night. Miriam had said she would stay up and meet her mother.

When Agnes looked at her watch and rose to go, Edward said, "I will get my things."

Agnes was upset. She gave him a quick hug and said, "No, Edward. They won't let you out."

She fled down the long hall and across the courtyard as fast as her short legs and heavy feet would let her. She did not stop until she reached the train station. She sat on a wooden bench and looked at her watch. She was an hour early. She could have spent more time with Edward. She felt guilty. By the time she got home, she had a cold. Miriam not only met her, but she had the kettle on the boil, and had put two hot water bottles in her mother's bed. Agnes could not talk, but she squeezed Miriam's hand.

CHAPTER 27

Autumn, 1915

Charles had had a long chat with Agnes, trying to think through what he thought and felt about the war. He saw through the patriotic lies in church and in the press, which Agnes did not, but the casualty lists in the papers did not lie, and a daily stream of wounded soldiers came by train to St. Chad's Anglican College, now a veterans' hospital. Charles visited the veterans regularly, taking them cake and fudge and Turkish delights made by Agnes and the girls. He felt more comfortable with them than with his colleagues at the bank. He hated the way his bank was prospering from the sale of Victory Bonds, his manager openly hoping that the war would not end, they were making so much money. Yet among the returned men at St. Chad's, Charles sensed a bitterness towards himself, that he might have relieved them, saved them, and he had not.

But Charles was not willing to kill any other human being. He joined up in the medical corps and felt right, he told Agnes, when he made that decision.

He was immediately called up and sent for basic training to Valcartier, Quebec. Deborah saw him off at the crowded station. They had to wait on the platform until wounded soldiers were unloaded. Deborah could not look. She stared at Charles's luggage, his kit bag, sensing the emptiness they promised her. She cried. Charles put his arm around her. She pulled away from the scratchiness, the smell of his tight khaki serge uniform.

"*I could not love thee dear so much, loved I not honour more,*" he quoted to her.

"Charles, let's get married when you come back," Deborah said.

Charles was startled. That seemed an improvident, risky thing to do. He got on the train without answering her.

Charles plummeted to the bottom of the social scale, with the wages of an unskilled laborer. In Montreal he was refused entry to a good restaurant because he was in a private's uniform. At Valcartier, after the senseless marches, the waiting in line after line, hour after hour, the sleeping with twenty noisy others in a tent, the eating slop from a tin, he thought only of holding Deborah's small breasts in his hands in front of the fire in 2929, then entering her, and staying inside her for the rest of his life. Despite his great drop in pay, he wrote to Deborah and said, "Yes, let's risk everything and get married when I get home." He looked at the word *home* and realized that Deborah would become his home.

After Charles had been a week in training in the sandy wasteland that was Valcartier, those in power discovered that he was a minister's son. He was chosen for officer training. He asked for twenty-four hours to think it over. That reply was not well received. He was warned that hesitation to receive such a promotion would go on his record. He said he still needed time to weigh the pros and cons. He could see it would make his life easier, for he was appalled at how he lost his dignity, his independence as an enlisted man. He felt treated like an animal. But he was also appalled at the quality of the commissioned officers. He did not want to be one of them.

After supper, to escape the cursing, the gambling, the constant singing of *"Pack Up Your Troubles," "Mademoiselle from Armentières"* and *"Tipperary,"* Charles followed a trail through scrub to a distant ridge. In a rocky hollow at the top of the ridge he came across a handsome sergeant-major smoking, his hat and jacket off. Charles saluted, and Leon J. Van Gorder smiled.

"No need to salute up here, soldier," he said. "No one can see us. Come sit on this dry rock with me. There's lots of room. Did you come to catch the sunset?"

Charles looked at the gold rimming the luminous western clouds, and sat beside Van. He was offered a cigarette, but he shook his head. "Yes, I miss the prairie skies."

"There's nothing like them, is there? Where are you from?"

"Regina." Charles noticed how easily he had said that, although he had spent most of his life in the east.

"I'm from Saskatchewan too," Van said. "I have a homestead north of Maidstone, but I thought I'd try this for a change. You get tired of poverty living on a farm. It wears you down. What were you doing for a living?"

"I was an accountant in the Northwest Bank. Doing quite well, actually. But here I am.... D'you mind my asking...how do you feel about being a non-commissioned officer? I ask this, because they offered me officer training this morning. I said I would have to think it over."

Van laughed. "They wouldn't be pleased that you did-n't jump at it. I would have."

"D'you mind if I think out loud, or are you supposed to be consorting with the likes of me?"

"Well, if no one catches us, it doesn't matter, does it?" Van stretched out his long legs, then clasped them to him again. "To answer your question...your name is?...Charles, if it's a non-commissioned rank they offered you, you're neither flesh, fish, nor good red herring. And you do all the work and take all the blame. The commissioned ones seem to know nothing, and they are treated like lords. I would-n't mind that for a while before I go back to the farm – a personal servant to dress and feed you, clean beds with sheets, and oh, do they eat well, with white table cloths and food we can only buy on the black market.... People call me Van, by the way, but I would prefer if you didn't."

It was Charles's turn to laugh. It was unthinkable that he would harm anyone knowingly. He outlined his pros and cons of applying for a commission, ending with the observation, "The men hate most of the officers so. I would hate to be so hated!"

Van lit another cigarette and looked off to the north. "That way madness lies, at least I think so, Charles. You're only going to be with these men for a few months. Let's face it, most of them will get killed. So will the officers, anyone who gets sent over there. That's what's been hap-pening. But you have to live with yourself for the rest of your life. You have to make decisions you can live with."

That principle was familiar and congenial to Charles. "But when I go over, with whatever rank, I'm likely to be killed and there will be no rest of my life."

"That's what's been happening."

"Then it's important to me who I die with, and

although I don't like the cursing and gambling and covert drinking I see in my tent, I wouldn't want to spend my short life in the company of men who are waited on, who are pampered, when others do the work."

"It's your choice, and whichever way you choose, you'll have regrets. Do you have a girl you are leaving behind?"

"Yes, I've just become engaged. I'm going to be married on embarkation leave!" Charles had told someone else.

Charles went to see his parents and his sister in Kingston before going back to Regina. His sister was aloof as always, having a very full social life and being newly engaged to an officer. His mother was proud that he had joined up at last. She wished he had chosen to have a commission. There were many questions about Deborah and her family. Charles's mother guessed she would be a great beauty. Charles was evasive. His mother was determined to come to the wedding, but Charles protested there wasn't time for a proper wedding, there would only be Deborah, himself, and witnesses.

Charles's father was quiet and anxious. Charles took him for a long walk down to the Market Place then along the lake shore. He was able to ask his father what attracted him to the ministry. His father stopped, stared at the stump of a maple that had been broken off by lightning but still produced slim branches with leaves beginning to rust. He gave an ironic laugh. "No one has asked me that before," he said. But he was still thinking as they walked, and Charles gave him time. "I suppose, looking back, that I failed into it. I love the classics and wanted to be a classics professor, but I didn't have the marks to go on. My mother wanted one of her sons to go into the church, so I became that one. There was no calling, no great conversion on the way to Damascus. It was a job."

Unprepared for his father's frankness, Charles stared across the choppy water of Lake Ontario, then turned and embraced his father. It felt like embracing the trunk of the maple tree, rigid, not used to being touched. *Oh, this must change*, Charles thought. *We can't live lives of quiet desperation.* "I love you, Father," he said.

Charles's father burst into tears, then wiped them away with a folded handkerchief. "Come back to us, Charles," he said. "Take care of yourself in that wicked war. The world needs men like you. I'm proud of you."

It was Charles's turn to cry, and he wiped his tears on his father's handkerchief. They walked back arm in arm, Charles determined to share his life with his father.

CHAPTER 28

Spring, 1916

Spring comes gently to Regina. There is no crack of ice breaking and thundering down a river as in Winnipeg. The sun warms the sting in the air. Then the snow seems to sigh and melt, revealing dandelions and crocusses in the brown winter grass. Water runnels under and beside the wooden sidewalks.

Such was the awakening of Jessie Jackson. As her breasts began to bud then fill, deep long dimples appeared in her cheeks. Louis was the first to notice, then watch Jessie's unfolding beauty. Miriam had been the tall, dark, almost aloof beauty of the family, but now Jessie was tall, fair, rounded, confident, her loveliness releasing an exuberance in her, a readiness to laugh, to skate, to go on long walks with Kitty Taylor. She sometimes wore Miriam's cast-off dresses – Agnes worried that they were too mature for a girl of sixteen – but Miriam and Deborah were so pleased with the beauty of their sister that also they made and bought her dresses.

Agnes was grateful that Jessie was not going to be her ugly duckling, but she worried about the exuberance, calling it silliness. Jessie had begun to curl her brown hair in rags and wrap it around her head the way her sisters did. She would no longer read to her mother or do homework at the dining table while her mother and Miriam wrote their daily letters. Jessie said she had done her homework at school. In fact, she had stopped going to school, and she and Kitty spent their days in the Glasgow House department store or the Regina Trading Company. Miriam alerted her mother to Jessie's not attending school.

Jessie was going out one evening, her skates over her shoulder. She and Kitty hoped to catch one more evening of skating before the ice turned to slush.

"Put those skates away, Madam. You aren't going anywhere," Agnes called from the dining room.

Jessie flounced into the dining room, whining.

"Now, what's this about your not attending school for two weeks?"

"I'm not going back, and neither is Kitty."

Agnes had already talked to the school principal. He said Jessie was disinterested in learning at this point. "You can lead a horse to water, but you can't make him drink, Mrs. Jackson."

Agnes was devastated. For the first time the family could afford to have a child graduate, and this silly ninnie wouldn't do it. But there was no forcing her. Agnes decided to send her to business school so that she'd earn more money than being a clerk in a store.

"Well, it's Pitman's for you, Madam. You and I will go there tomorrow."

Jessie cried. She wanted to work in a department store in women's dresses.

She went to Pitman's Business School.

When the Jackson girls were young, Deborah, the oldest, had been the queen when they played. Now that she was the first to marry, she became the queen again. She had fairy tale plans for her wedding. She wanted to have invitations printed in silver ink and sent to..."Who shall I send invitations to, Ma?" she asked. Agnes's eyebrows shot up. They had no close friends in Regina, and she disapproved of sending invitations to England, the war making it impossible for anyone to come. And to send a silver-printed invitation to Fannie and George on the farm? She and Miriam persuaded Deborah to dispense with the invitations. They also persuaded her that in wartime it would be inappropriate to have a large wedding or a dress that she could not wear again. But Agnes and Miriam did give up knitting for the troops to work on satin and lace for Deborah's trousseau, and Agnes got out her Mrs. Beaton recipe book to cook a cake. It was a small wedding in St. Paul's church, with only the extended family attending, followed by an ample supper around the dining table.

Deborah's wedding and Jack's letters were an anguish to Miriam. She often cried. His letters were ardent. He dreamed of holding Miriam naked in his arms, kissing her body all over. He wanted to have children, to hold them in his arms. Where would she like to live? Around the corner from her mother on Retallack or Robinson? Miriam trembled when she scanned the casualty lists every day.

After the shock of the second battle of Ypres where Jack Foxxe was wounded, the war took a desperate turn. The Allies were not winning, and casualty lists filled the local newspapers. Parliament in Ottawa was fighting for and against conscription. There had been no shortage of recruits in the west for two years. All quotas had been filled immediately. Louis, who couldn't resist volunteering, had been turned down because of his height. Now there were no limits and recruiting officers were everywhere in Regina. Women wore black, wounded veterans wore bright blue. Billboards appeared showing Lord Kitchener pointing and saying, *"Your king calls you. How will you answer him?"* or *"Do help Tommy Aitkins."*

With Charles overseas, Deborah looked for ways to express her patriotism. She enlisted Jessie – she knew that Miriam would tell her mother – to collect white feathers from the geese in the back garden. On Sunday afternoon, when her mother was having her bath, they took a tray of them and handed them out to men who were not in uniform, asking why not. Jessie was full of enthusiasm. They spent two hours handing out feathers in Victoria Square. When they came home, the table was set for dinner. They placed a feather under the water glasses of Arnold, Louis, and Billy.

When the whole family was seated for dinner – Edward and Charles's chairs were against the wall – and Agnes was carving up the prairie chickens the men had brought home, Arnold was the first to pick up his white feather.

"So what's this all about?" he asked the table.

Louis and Billy picked up their feathers and looked stunned.

Agnes glanced around the table and took in what was happening. She dropped the carving knife. Her glare settled on Deborah and Jessie, who had lost their enthusiasm. "Leave this table. Leave this house if you don't know how to behave," she said.

Jessie looked like a muskrat cornered by a bright light. She followed Deborah in standing, then in going upstairs.

Agnes walked around the table and collected the feathers. She put them in the cookstove, came back and said, "Now get it into you before it gets cold."

Miriam, smelling the burning feathers, stood, then followed her sisters up to their bedroom.

"She hates us," Deborah wailed, sitting on the ecru cover Agnes had crocheted for the double bed. "She has never loved us or wanted us. We're just servants to her. We pay board. Why can't we say or do anything without her permission?"

"Oh, I think she does love us in her North-of-England way," Miriam said, sitting beside Deborah and putting an arm around her.

Jessie stared at her sisters. "What d'you mean, North-of-England way?" she asked. "Either you love your children, or you don't."

"Well, she doesn't show it in an affectionate way," Miriam said. "They don't. They cover up their feelings. I think she thinks it would bring bad luck. But she's *loyal* to us and has been good at cooking and sewing and keeping a clean house for us."

"She's too hard on us," Jessie said.

"Well, she's hard on herself too. I think she believes that soft people go under." Miriam sighed. "We'll just have to be more affectionate to our children."

The mention of children made Deborah cry. As Miriam wiped her eyes, she said, "I miss Charles so, and he's so unhappy being away from me."

"We were only copying Mother's heroine," Jessie said.

"What d'you mean?"

"It was in the paper. Mrs. Pankhurst is handing out white feathers in London."

Miriam felt anger spurt through her. She went downstairs to the dining room and announced, "Mrs. Pankhurst has been handing out white feathers in London. The girls thought you would be pleased, that it was the patriotic thing to do."

Agnes's face flamed, and she stood to confront Miriam. "She has not! She would not!"

"Oh, but she has," Arnold said. "It's in the English papers. She's been touring the country handing them out." He offered a cigarette to Louis and Billy. No one felt much like eating.

"Well, I'll have to see that to believe it. You men, you are loyal sons of the Empire, doing a good job, each one of you, and I don't want..." She broke down. "I don't want you going off to war." But they did.

Louis and Billy were going to a rugby game that night. Arnold decided to join them, rather than be at home with his mother and sisters. He had difficulty following the game. It didn't matter about the Pankhurst feathers. Conscription was looming. Better to jump than be pushed. And Arnold had not improved his job situation. Both of the farm implements companies had offered him jobs as a travelling salesman. He was not willing to leave his home and friends in Regina. He stayed where he was, clerking in the hardware store, but he was restless.

After the Regina team had trounced the Moose Jaw team, the three men flocked with a singing, yelling crowd to join the players in drinking beer, then followed the drunken team members to the recruiting table of the 195th Battalion. Louis led the three, as the army had cut the standard of height and chest measurements to include men of Louis' size. He pointed to a crude poster that promised *"The 195th Battalion will train you, feed you, arm you and give you a chance to shoot Germans. What more could any healthy young man want?"*

"What more could any healthy young man want?" Louis repeated.

"Let's sign up as waggon drivers. You can handle horses, Louis," Arnold said. But the recruiting officer said there was no need for waggon drivers this year and urged Infantry. The young men withdrew and lit cigarettes. "Anything but the Poor Bloody Infantry," Arnold said. "They don't last a week. Artillery, Engineers, or Army Medical Corps. But we stick together or we don't go." They agreed on Engineers.

Arnold was too high-spirited to notice himself signing an oath *To honestly and faithfully defend His Majesty King George the Fifth, his Heirs and Successors, in Person, Crown, and Dignity, against all enemies, observe and obey all orders of His Majesty, His Heirs and Successors, and of all the Generals and Officers set over me. So help me God.*

What Arnold did notice was that Billy had called himself Billy Jackson and gave Agnes as his next of kin. *My mother will be surprised when she learns of this, if she learns of this,* Arnold mused. He wondered if Billy had been calling himself Jackson in all his job applications. Well, why not? With Edward out of the picture, he was able to claim Agnes as a dependent. That would soften the blow when she found her table empty except for the girls.

The table was empty of men within a week. For their last meal together Agnes killed the two white geese and served them to the family.

Louis gave Jessie a silver embossed box filled with chocolates.

CHAPTER 29

Spring, 1916

When the men had gone off to a rugby game and the washing up was done, Agnes went to the front porch where the newpapers sat folded. She perused the *Manchester Guardian*s for news of Mrs. Pankhurst, then sat until dark, her insides churning.

After she went upstairs, knelt to say her prayers, and climbed into her cold bed, Agnes lay awake all night. Around the dark room, lit only by the street light, the image of Mrs. Pankhurst floated, beautiful as ever, gracious, friendly. That was how she had been when she first came into the shop in 1894, admiring the freshness of the produce, ordering generously, buying imported fruits. Brother Bob, who did the deliveries, said the Pankhursts had moved into a substantial house in Victoria Park. The Jacksons were still living in Edward's substantial house in Rusholme. Mrs. Pankhurst continued to come into the shop in the Wilmslow Road to place her order, to address Agnes as "Mrs. Jackson."

At the urging of other chapel members, Agnes had gone to hear Keir Hardie speak. Keir Hardie, the Independent

Labour Party leader, the self-educated Ayrshire Miners' Secretary, had worked from the age of seven. Agnes caught her breath. With only two years of schooling, she felt uneducated, but this man, with no formal education, was addressing a large crowd. His personal warmth and straight speaking appealed to Agnes. He was a teetotaller, he said, not to spoil people's fun, but to put food on the tables of the poor. He said the only way to change society was to give women the vote, some control over their lives. That phrase grabbed Agnes. She repeated it to herself, "some control over their lives." That's what she had lost when she married. It was as if she didn't exist. Edward made all the decisions in the house, and he gambled on the racehorses. Oh, how he gambled and lost.

After the meeting Agnes did the boldest thing in her life – she signed up and paid up – the Independent Labour Party. To her surprise, Mrs. Pankhurst, elegantly dressed, was behind her to sign up.

"Mrs. Jackson, may I present my husband, Dr. Pankhurst?"

Agnes straightened and shook hands. She was glad she was wearing her Sunday best and her cameo brooch. She liked handsome Dr. Pankhurst. They took her to meet Keir Hardie. He had a long white beard, not trimmed like Edward's. He talked openly. He asked Dr. Pankhurst about his friend, John Stuart Mill, the author of the Woman Suffrage Bill and of the Married Women's Property Act. Agnes felt accepted by these three, an acceptance she felt only at her chapel.

In 1898 Dr. Pankhurst had suddenly died, leaving Mrs. Pankhurst few means to raise five children. She moved to a small detached house at 63 Nelson Street, and turned her front room into a shop where she sold what Bob described as "bric-a-brac." Agnes noticed that she now ordered inexpensive local produce at the shop, but Agnes did not see her for five years. Those were the years when Agnes's infant son, Franklin, then her eight-year-old Stanley, died of diphtheria.

In October of 1903 Bob had brought a note from Mrs. Pankhurst to Agnes. It asked her to tea the next day "to discuss some exciting ideas." Agnes had two servants at the time. It was easy for her to get away.

Mrs. Pankhurst had led Agnes through her front room shop, filled with Chinese teapots, Japanese embroidery, Indian brasses and William Morris cretonnes. She said, "So you see we are both shop keepers, Mrs. Jackson. It's a hard life, isn't it?" A handful of women sat in the small side parlour, two of them clearly mill workers in dark, plain dresses. Christabel Pankhurst, with wildly pencilled eyebrows, much more forceful than her mother, spoke against the caution of the new Labour Party and the existing radical suffragist movement, The North of England Society, which held garden parties and did not include trade unions or textile workers or Labour politicians. She wanted to form a new political organization to militate for votes for women, and her mother supported her. Agnes knew nothing of the politics of the situation. She was still grieving the loss of her two sons, but she admired and trusted Mrs. Pankhurst. She became a founding member of the Women's Social and Political Union.

When Christabel Pankhurst asked for volunteers to speak at meetings, Agnes recoiled. Not only must Edward not know that she was out of the house, except to go to church meetings, but she was by nature a private person. She would never speak in public, even to ask a question. One of the mill workers, Mrs. Hannah Mitchell, volun-

teered to speak at Agnes's church, the Primitive Methodist
Chapel in Moss Lane. Agnes was assigned to go with her, to
support her.

Hannah Mitchell was a sharp-featured young woman
with a Derbyshire village accent. Like Agnes, smiling was
unfamiliar to her. Life had been too harsh for her to learn
to smile or laugh. When she met Agnes at Whitworth Park,
she was trembling. Only her conviction that the distribution of wealth was unfair forced her to speak out in public.
Agnes worried that she would not find her voice at all, she
trembled so. Agnes tucked her well-fleshed arm under
Hannah Mitchell's spare one. But when Hannah was introduced, and admitted her nervousness, it vanished, and she
spoke ardently for the cause of working women, particularly those in the Lancashire cotton mills. The audience
stood and cheered. Colour rose through Hannah Mitchell's
neck. She managed a frozen smile.

Agnes took Hannah Mitchell to a tea shop in the
Wilmslow Road. Over tea and scones they became like girls tittering over Hannah's success. With food Hannah opened up.
She ate with relish, crumbs clinging to her lips, yet seeming
unaware of the food except as fuel for her mind. Agnes ordered
more tea and scones and jam. Hannah had had only two
weeks of formal schooling before her mother took her out of
school to be the family drudge. Agnes had had two years at a
local dame school before she became her mother's drudge. But
then, she had been rescued by her father and put into the shop.
Hannah had run away from home, and ended up a mill worker married to a Socialist. She had one son and wanted no more
children. She did not see them, as Agnes did, as expansions of
herself. Hannah wanted time to read, to walk in the fresh air.

When the Pankhursts heard of Hannah Mitchell's success, she was assigned speech after speech for two years,

Agnes to be her support. That support was needed. Men heckled her. Boys wearing 'Christian Endeavour' badges threw eggs and tomatoes. But the hostile crowds brought larger crowds than orderly ones did. Over tea Agnes and Hannah would mock the men who had mocked them.

"Go home and wash the pots," Agnes would say.

"Go whoam an mind yer babbies," Hannah would say.

"Wot about the old man's kippers?" They would laugh. It was a fulfilling time. The movement flourished.

Two years later, October 13, 1905, the founding members were asked to attend a political rally at the Free Trade Hall, the speakers to be Liberal politicians Winston Churchill and Sir Edward Grey. Agnes waited outside the hall for Hannah, who had had to bring her washing off the line and set out her husband's supper before coming. They had to stand at the packed meeting. Agnes was caught up in the speeches – the candidates spoke so well. At question time, Annie Kenny stood up and with her working class accent shouted, "Will the Liberal government give votes to women?" When she was ignored, Christabel Pankhurst, beside her, stood up, repeating the question. Then the two women unfurled a banner, *"Votes for Women."* They were hustled out of the hall, past Agnes and Hannah, who followed them. Christabel spat at the policeman who had her arms pinned. The two women were taken off to the police station where Christabel chose seven days in Strangeways prison rather than pay a fine. Hannah found words as she and Agnes walked away. "Good for them," she said. Agnes walked on in silence, troubled. The look on the policeman's face haunted her. *If we all spat on policeman, where would we be?* she asked herself.

"What other women do, I can do," Hannah said grimly as they parted....

When Hannah served her seven days in prison, Agnes

supported her as best she could without Edward learning where she was going. Hannah was devastated by the ill-treatment, the bad food in prison. "It's all right for you, Mrs. Jackson. You have your servants to prepare the meals and do the work. But if I don't cook, no one eats in our house. And there will be a load of washing to greet me when I get home." She was weak and ill.

It was not true that Agnes still had servants. The Jacksons had lost them and the house in Rusholme and the fruit store to Edward's gambling. They now lived in a rented house in the Wilmslow Road. When Agnes was not cook, housemaid and nursemaid, she was relieving Edward and Bob in the greengrocer shop, the only source of support for a family of seven. But Agnes did not want to detract from Hannah's sacrifice by complaining about her reduced circumstances.

A crisis developed in the WSPU. It became clear that the Pankhursts were fighting for a Women with Property Act, which meant that all the working class women, married or single, who owned nothing, would not be franchised. Hannah and some of the women asked for democratic elections in the WSPU. The Pankhursts refused. Hannah left the movement. Agnes supported the Pankhursts – they were the logical women to lead, and being ladies, they would get more attention in the conservative press. Agnes continued to pay her membership, but she too became inactive. She had four surviving children to look after. But she remained loyal to Mrs. Pankhurst, and read with admiration in *The Suffragette* her many imprisonments and hunger strikes in the struggle for woman suffrage, now suspended because of the war.

But this handing out of white feathers to young men in civilian clothes! What was Mrs. Pankhurst thinking of?

Agnes had read that Mrs. Pankhurst's only son had died of infantile paralysis. So she had no sons at the front to make her bitter. Why was she trying to force other women's sons into crippling or death?

Agnes wrote next day to Hannah Mitchell and enclosed the letter in a food parcel to her friend Nellie Bowich, hoping Mrs. Bowich could readdress the letter to Hannah Mitchell in north Manchester.

> *My dear friend,*
>
> *You will be surprised to hear from me from half way across the world and half way across Canada, but this is where life has brought me and my family. We could not make a decent living in the Old Country, and are doing so now, even with this dreadful war.*
>
> *I have thought of you often as England suffers losses and food shortages. If I hear from you I will gladly pack a food bundle from our Canadian plenty.*
>
> *But that is not what has prompted me to write. No, I write to apologize for not seeing your wisdom and that of Mrs. Despard and Mrs. Selina Cooper in dropping out of the WSPU when Mrs. Pankhurst and her daughters did not agree to democratic elections. At the time I was charmed by their appeal, by their dramatic sacrifices, and, let me be honest, by their status as ladies. I thought it would help our cause to be led by such distinguished women. I was mistaken, and I ask your forgiveness for not following you and the other fine women who broke away and formed the Women's International League for Peace and*

Freedom rather than support leaders who were not elected.

Now I read in the Guardian that Mrs. Emmeline Pankhurst – she who has no sons! – has been handing out white feathers to men whose lives she knows nothing about. How humiliating for them! How presumptuous of her! The militant suffragettes now supporting militarism, conscription for men and women, (but not the Pankhurst women, I'll wager!) and internment of all people of enemy race.

Please accept my apology for my error in judgment, my dear friend. I so valued your company in the work that we did together for our cause, and I much admired your ability to face those hostile crowds and to speak the truth clearly and with conviction.

If you can find the time to write to your old friend, I would be most grateful to hear from you. And I should join your organization. At least I can make a financial contribution. We are getting the vote here in Canada without having to fight for it. Everyone's energy is taken up by this dreadful war.

Affectionately,
Agnes Jackson

CHAPTER 30

June, 1916

Dear Arnold,

This letter is for you alone. I have written my letter to Deborah and one to your mother thanking her for a wonderful parcel.

We have always known that men fail into the military from lack of success in civilian life – including, and probably especially the officers. Why do we put our lives in the hands of men who obey men equally limited in intelligence?

I am seeing men being slaughtered by the thousands after being ordered to take with rifles a hill full of German machine guns. If they refuse such idiocy, their platoon comrades are forced to shoot them, then parade past their bodies. Our troops are constantly sent over the top as shooting ducks for the Germans who stay under cover.

It is madness. Terror. We are in a hell created by madmen and we can't escape.

But you can, Arnold. Fight conscription! Refuse to enlist! And <u>do not let Louis and Billy sign up.</u> It's certain death.

Look after Deborah for me. I will get this letter past censorship somehow.

Fraternally,
Charles

CHAPTER 31

August, 1916

With her young men off in the war, Agnes had to take over the gardening. She had never gardened before, but she seemed to have absorbed what to do by watching Edward when she went out to get eggs or vegetables or raspberries. First the geese and now the dog kept the ground squirrels from eating the produce.

Agnes was in the front garden weeding around the brown-eyed susans – weeding the weeds, Arnold would say – how she missed his terse comments – when Deborah came down Twelfth Avenue, home from work. Agnes stared at the shape of her daughter, the walk.

"Is there something you want to tell me?" she asked Deborah.

"Yes, I'm tired and hungry. Is supper ready?"

Agnes sighed. "Yes, everything's ready. Shouldn't we wait for Miriam and Jessie to come from work?"

"I'm going to make myself a cup of tea," Deborah said, walking into the house.

After supper Agnes said to Miriam, who was washing the dishes, "Miriam, could it be that Deborah is pregnant?"

"It could be," Miriam said. "She hasn't said."

It occurred to both women that Deborah might not know.

"I'll ask her." Miriam sighed that she had to take over her mother's responsibilities again. Miriam had often stayed with a favourite aunt in England who had talked about the reproductive system with her.

"Not in front of Jessie."

"Why not? She has to learn about life. Better sooner than later."

With the men away at war, the young women had each taken a room. Deborah was in the one with the double bed. Miriam knocked on the door and went in. Deborah was lying on the bed reading Charles's letters. Miriam sat on the corner of the bed, looking at photos of the royal family that Deborah had cut out of magazines, framed with tin foil from tea packages, and hung around the room.

"Deborah, Mother thinks you might be pregnant. Are you?"

"Don't be so silly."

"Well, it does happen when you're married, you know.... When did you have the curse last?"

"Oh, I can't keep track of that kind of thing. Really, Miriam, you are prying, you know." Deborah turned on her side, her back to Miriam.

"Yes, but it would be awkward if a baby popped out of you while you were at work, or if your employer gave you notice because he had noticed your shape."

"What do you mean, a baby popped out?"

When Miriam explained as best she could, Deborah

burst into tears. She was four months pregnant. She developed morning sickness the next morning, and gave up her job before she was fired. Deborah was reluctant to tell Charles about her pregnancy. "He'll be so mad at me!" she wailed.

Miriam smiled to herself. "It might give him something to live for, something to come back to."

"What's wrong with me?" Deborah demanded.

Caught, Miriam said, "Well, there would just be more of you for him to love, for both of you to love." She realized she was suggesting the irrational to Deborah. And yet, if she had become pregnant, she would have something of Jack to love in this long, dangerous absence.

With the men away, Miriam walked the dog out on the prairie before breakfast and after supper, enjoying the time to herself and the undemanding company of Roger. She now persuaded Deborah to walk in the evenings after dark so that no one would notice Deborah's condition, and Jessie took her to the moving pictures to see Mary Pickford and the Gish sisters until Agnes decided that Deborah was too large to be seen, even in the dark.

Deborah became the queen again. Her mother and her two sisters bought muslin and flannelette to sew for the baby, one at the machine, the other two doing the hemming. Deborah read their tea leaves to them. She always saw a letter on its way or good fortune.

Deborah's baby did not just pop out of her navel as Deborah had expected. It was a three day labour, and Deborah screamed her pain and terror. Agnes said brusquely of her pain, "It's soon forgotten, Deborah. Women have the shortest memories." After work, Miriam sat with Deborah, holding her hands and wiping her forehead.

When the doctor delivered a wailing healthy boy, Agnes

asked, "Is he sound of wind and limb?" She looked at the child and walked away.

"You seem not pleased with him," Miriam said to her mother over tea in the living room. "We need more men in the family."

"Boys are weaker than girls. Men are weaker than women," Agnes said, staring at the fire. The baby looked like her Franklin, who had died in infancy.

Deborah called the baby Lawrence Bennington.

"Bennington? Bennington? What kind of name is that?" Agnes asked. "It's not one of our family names. Is it one of Charles's?"

"I just like the sound of it. It sounds so distinguished."

Agnes was cleaning Lawrence Bennington, after changing his nappie. "Well, Mr. Bennington, we won't expect you to fill your nappies any more like other babies, will we?"

When she came home from work, Jessie took over the baby. He was like a doll come to life.

But when Jessie and Miriam were at work, it was Agnes who was nurse as well as cook, housekeeper, and gardener. She used to say of her friend Mrs. Bowich's housekeeping, "We could live on what she wastes." With one income less coming into the household, Agnes fed her daughters frugally from what she could grow, from the cheapest cuts of meat, and from frozen pike she bought at the door. She was always one to put pastry on meat or to bury it in a suet pudding to make it go further. She would-n't kill the chickens until they were past egg laying. Then she made vast quantities of chicken soup, and chicken pies when it was cold enough for them to keep in the cold pantry.

When Agnes showed irritability with looking after the baby, Deborah decided she would take the baby east to stay with his grandparents in Kingston. Charles had wanted his father to christen the baby, had wanted her to visit his family. Agnes did not think the baby should travel on the train with all its germs, but Deborah was adamant. Well, she will have to take over as mother to this child sometime, Agnes reasoned. With the trains requisitioned for troop movements, Deborah stayed in Kingston for the rest of the war.

CHAPTER 32

Fall, 1916

When the leader of the new Canadian Corps, Arthur Currie, saw the battlefield in daylight, he gasped in horror. The Somme had been chosen by Haig as a great improvement on the flat, muddy plains of Flanders. But Haig had not visited the site, as he hadn't the Ypres Salient. Originally it had been treed chalky downs, but by September when the Canadians had been transferred to it, it had become a grassless, treeless quagmire of shell holes filled with water from the autumn rains, the only organic matter being the visible legs and skulls of the dead. It stank of excrement. 20,000 British had been slain the first day, 600 Newfoundlanders. The two and a half months that followed saw the bloodiest fighting in history, with no strategic advantage gained. Mindless orders were given to attack hopeless objectives. Men were being killed faster than graves could be dug, their bodies buried in mass graves with quicklime between layers. Why persist in this madness? Why add the fresh Canadian troops to this slaughter? Currie went to see Haig and said he wanted no part of it. He was warned of insubordination and given objectives to attack and take. Although Canada had contributed nearly half a million troops, Prime Minister Borden was not part of the decision-making until after this five-month battle, when, threatening withdrawal of Canadian troops, he insisted.

To get to the Somme front from Ypres, Charles was packed for hours in a boxcar on the French railway marked *"Hommes 40, chevaux 8."* The railroads were inadequate to the movement of millions of men. Trains were backed up for six miles. The road surfaces were chewed up by heavy lorries trying to move supplies to the front. Despite kits weighing eighty pounds, the Canadian reinforcements, having won Mount Sorrel at a terrible cost, were in high spirits, singing and joking. When they got off the train at Albert in rain, they sobered. The Australian troops they were relieving at Pozieres marched past them like ghosts, their faces stricken. No jokes in passing.

Being a medical aid, Charles was sometimes stationed in a dressing station behind the lines, to be called after a battle to look among the dead for the rifles of the wounded stuck upright in the ground beside them. But at other times, led by the chaplain, he went over the top with the men in the second wave and applied dressings to the wounded. Charles admired the padre in this unit, Allan Frampton from Regina, not only for his courage, but for his devotion to the men. Charles found himself taking communion again and assisting Allan in serving communion.

When a box arrived from England full of Books of Common Prayer, Charles had taken one and browsed in it during his periods of rest and recovery. He loved the language of the liturgy, but he was shocked by the Catechism passages. Had he really vowed as an adolescent, *To renounce the devil and all his works, the pomps and vanities of this wicked world, and all the sinful lusts of the flesh?* Had he really vowed to *Honour and obey the king and all that are put in authority under him? To order myself lowly and reverently to all my betters?* Douglas Haig was *the devil and all his works,* and submitting themselves to all their *betters* was how all these strong, fine men got slaughtered. Charles saw it clearly. The church was an instrument for controlling men to do what those in power wanted to do to increase their wealth and power.

Then Charles realized that when he signed up he signed an attestation swearing *Obedience to the king, his heirs and successors, and such generals and officers as the king might place over them.* He was no better than a child. Had he learned *nothing* since he was a child, signing his life away the way he had done?

Allan Frampton, the padre, was fatally wounded. There being no one else alive who could do it, Charles read the burial service over him. He chose

> *Lord, thou hast been our refuge*
> *from one generation to another.*
> *Before the mountains were brought forth*
> *or ever the earth and the world were made*
> *thou art God from everlasting, and world without end.*
> *Thou turnest man to destruction:*
> *again thou sayest, Come again ye children of men.*
> *For a thousand years in thy sight are but as yesterday:*
> *seeing that is past like a watch in the night.*
> *As soon as thou scatterest them, they are even as a sleep*
> *and fade away suddenly like the grass.*
> *In the morning it is green, and groweth up*
> *but in the evening it is cut down, dried up and withered...*

> *Now is Christ risen from the dead*

and become the first fruits of them that slept.
For since by man came death
by man came also the resurrection of the dead.

Charles took Allan's place until a replacement came. Before the men were sent over the top Allan had read the passage from Mark, *"And he asked him, what is thy name? And he answered saying, My name is Legion: for we are many,"* and had led the men over the top chanting the twenty-third psalm. Charles did the same, but after a battle, while he worked covered in the blood of the wounded and dying, he would be consumed by rage.

After a month of fighting in rain, sleet and mud, the remnants of the first, second, and third Canadian divisions were sent back to Vimy on October 17th to refit and replace the casualties. Every second infantryman had been killed. It seemed to the survivors that horses, vehicles and equipment were valued more than human lives. The men were expendable. The equipment not.

Charles was kept on with the other medical people to service the fourth division, which came from Ypres to replace their exhausted companions. The medical station was moved to Courcelette.

On October 30th it was the Princess Pats' turn to face engagement. The battlefield was an evil-smelling waste of stagnant, scummy water and mud, planks and duckboard the only roads over this slime. A madman had chosen this as a battlefield, was sending these men to fight in sleet and rain.

Lieutenant Jack Foxxe had been given part of the Regina Trench to recapture. *If I capture it, I will return to Regina to capture my love, if not...*Jack decided. He gave his men their rum and drank a tot with them. It didn't reach his cold wet feet, and he offered another tot to anyone who wanted it. One of the corporals began playing a mouth organ and some of the men sang, one or two heartily, most faintly. Others, their hands over their ears against the whine and shriek of the artillery bombardment that warned of their raid, crouched, staring in terror.

The bells of hell go ting-a-ling-a-ling
for you but not for me.
And the little devils sing-a-ling-a-ling
for you but not for me.
Oh Death, where is thy sting-a-ling-a-ling
Oh grave thy victory?
The devils of hell go ting-a-ling-a-ling
for you but not for me.

When Jack blew his whistle and led his men up the ladder, the fear he felt left him – he had his job to do – but he also knew his number was up, and he chanted to himself, "Oh Lord, into thy hands I commend my spirit."

After three days without sleep, Charles and other stretcher bearers were in no-man's-land at dusk rescuing the wounded. Trying to staunch blood pumping out of a shrapnel wound, Charles looked up to assess the situation. He recognized Jack Foxxe, his neck and shoulder being bandaged by a German stretcher bearer. When Charles finished dressing his patient, he went over to where the Germans were working and put a hand on the German's shoulder. "Danke, kamerade," he said, and gestured that they should exchange prisoners. The German was agreeable.

Charles put his face close to Jack's. "Are you all right, Regina chum?" he asked. "Do you think you and this soldier can walk to the dressing station?"

Jack Foxxe stared at Charles through clouded eyes and his mouth twitched sideways. Did he recognize Charles from 2929 where he had been happy? Jack struggled up, clinging to the German. Charles got the other wounded man on his feet, looped their arms together, and pointed the way along duckboards back to the line. He urged them to walk carefully, which was all their wounds allowed them to do.

The next day, among the dead, Charles found Jack Foxxe's body and that of the other soldier lying face down in mud, the sky reflected in a puddle beside them. They had suffocated.

When the fighting stopped from exhaustion and loss of life, Charles asked his dugout, "What are we doing entrusting our lives to a bunch of butchers?"

"We are lions led by donkeys," a soldier with a Yorkshire accent agreed.

Encouraged, Charles went on, "Wars have always been fought by the workers, who are always the losers." There was silence. "I hear whole French divisions are refusing to fight. Courage is the refusal to follow absurd orders."

"Knock it off, blow-hard," one man said.

Charles could be court-martialed for talking like this. But if he were shot, who would be given the job of shooting him? They would. No one reported him. There was no one left alive in the field to report him to.

Anger burned inside Charles day and night as he tended the obscenity of shattered bodies. He kept saying, "You're going to be all right, all right." But he knew he was wrong. He decided that if Douglas Haig came within shooting distance, he would grab someone's rifle and shoot him.

Then Agnes Jackson wrote to say his son was born, and above his consuming rage floated a small distant image of the future. He must fight to stay alive for his wife and child. He must live to build a better world.

CHAPTER 33

November, 1916

When John Foxxe knocked on the door of 2929 at dusk one day, Miriam knew who it was and what it was he had to tell her. With the relentless lists of casualties in the newspaper day after day, year after year, how could her Jack escape, when he had been there so long? And his pining letters had stopped coming.

John Foxxe looked wild and distraught as Agnes let him in. He looked for Miriam, and wrapped himself around her, sobbing. Miriam was calm as she held Jack's father in her arms. She had already cried herself empty. Agnes had gone to the kitchen and came back with a tea tray. Miriam led John to her father's chair, stirred the embers, and threw a piece of coal on the fire.

Jack Foxxe tried to drink tea, but he was trembling so the clatter of the cup was too much. He got out two telegrams, waving them. "His commanding officer said he died instantly and gallantly leading his men in battle," he said.

Miriam's instinct was now mistrust of what they were told by those in power. She had read and heard too much about the war. But it didn't matter. Her Jack was dead, and she was dead.

"Miriam, I don't know what to do for her, his mother. She's beside herself."

"You came in a car?" Agnes asked.

"Yes."

"We will come and give what comfort we can." Agnes went into the kitchen and packed a basket of food.

There was no comfort to assuage Mirabelle's grief. Unhappily she blamed her husband, who had his own grief to deal with.

Agnes called on Mirabelle daily when Miriam was at work. She took some little treat, then sat and knitted, so that Mirabelle could talk, blame, cry or be silent.

She was with Mirabelle when Jack's kit and personal effects arrived. When Mirabelle unpacked his hair brush, some of Jack's hair was tangled in the bristles. She sat with a comb in one hand, the brush in another, as if she was going to clean the brush for her son. But she didn't.

How to fill the emptiness in this house? Agnes looked around. The Foxxes had moved into a larger house than the one in Lakeview Miriam had seen. The new one was on Albert Street on the south side of the bridge. There was a square red Axminster carpet in the center of every room, somehow too small to unite the room, to make the new furniture look comfortable, to make the room look lived in. The house smelled of newness.

Agnes gradually introduced the idea that Julia, now pregnant by some soldier, Julia wasn't sure who, needed a home. At first Mirabel did not hear her, could not imagine sharing this empty space with the lively Romanian and a baby. But she did hear, and suddenly to have Julia and the child in the house seemed what she most wanted. There was a servant's room off the kitchen. Once the child, Alexander, was born and installed in the Albert Street House, John Foxxe began building an apartment onto the back of the house. In the short summers he began to garden and his wife joined him. John gave up his council work, his clubs. He could not deal with the condolences he received. He could not bear those whose sons were still alive. Mirabelle stayed with her Musical Society and the Assiniboia Club. She found being with women was a comfort. They accepted her without saying anything about her loss. They said, "I'm glad you could come," would squeeze her hand, and give her an occupation.

Comforting Miriam was another matter. She had become wooden, persisting in going to work, and doing her share of the work at home, but saying little. One evening when Jessie had gone to see Mary Pickford in the moving pictures, Miriam and Agnes sat by the fire sewing for the baby.

Agnes broke the silence they often worked in. "You know, your father and I were second best for each other," she said.

Miriam sewed on, wondering what she should say.

"I wonder if you know that your father was married before and his wife and child died in childbirth. It was a terrible blow to him." Agnes bit a thread with her teeth, drew another length of cotton from a spool, knotted it and threaded her needle. She dipped her needle into the hem of flannelette. "And I was engaged to be married...to a Chief Petty Officer in the merchant marine...Martin Smith...there, I've said his name after all these years, and it didn't hurt...I was young and brought up a Methodist. Well, he came home after six months on board ship...and he...got fresh with me." Agnes put down her work and smiled at the fire. "I can smile now, but in those days we were very proper and I knew nothing of men's passionate nature.... So that was the end of the engagement...."

Agnes left her work in her lap and stared at the fire.

"And you feel you would have been happier married to Martin?"

"No, for I wouldn't have had you children, and you are the joys of my life."

Miriam put down her work, walked over and hugged her mother across the wide stuffed chair. She suspected that her children meant the world to Agnes, but she had never been able to express her love for them by touching them.

"And your father and I...have been happy together. Before your two brothers died...that broke his heart. And before the economic depression...he couldn't cope with that. He's not a resourceful man, not a worker like my father. So he tried to make money by gambling...and it became a passion with him...we lost everything, and he must feel such a failure, so guilty to have done this to us."

"Because he loves you?"

"Because he loves us – his family, his home. I think what I'm trying to say is you will live again and love again. It's in your nature. But it will be different, and it may be the path you were meant to tread."

It was too soon to tell Miriam that. She heard her mother but she did not believe her.

She could not accept that Jack's life should end on a battlefield before he had lived it.

CHAPTER 34

Winter, 1916

Miriam was the only one to get mail from Arnold. Her mother sat watching her read. Her hands shook as she took each letter by him. Miriam let her keep the letters to reread.

> *Envelope: Note: Correspondence in this envelope need not be censored Regimentally. The contents are liable to examination at the Base.*
> *The following Certificate must be signed by the writer:-*
> <u>*I certify on my honour that the contents of this envelope refer to nothing but private and family matters.*</u>
> <u>*Signature (name only)*</u> *A.Jackson*

The letters and envelopes were written in pencil.

> *France*
> *Dear Miriam*
> > *I received your letter a little while ago and had*

intended writing sooner but didn't get down to it.

I came down from the line four days ago for a rest, and have had a fairly good time, lots of sleep, out in the open for a change after the foul air in a fritz dugout, and a cold bath in an animal trough and delousing. There is a canteen here where we can buy all sorts of things to eat, a thing we did-n't get a chance to do up the line, where if the rations are a little short you go hungry, but I have made that up since I came down. And green grass and leaves on the trees.

You would be surprised the difference it makes to a man, a couple of weeks up the line and he's pale and thin and looks worn out, for the want of sleep and the strain he is under while under fire but a few days back at the waggon lines and he is his old self again. Well you would hardly believe it but I ran across Charles last night. He came up to me while I was taking supper, I don't think I was so pleased to see anyone as I was to see him. He looks just the same as ever, only if anything a little older, his hair has gone gray, and he seems full of anger, and yet gentle. He says he wants to be a doctor when he comes home. He stayed here about two hours and then I walked on down the road a piece, he is about four miles away from here and that was his third trip up here to see me. I was up the line before, but he did see Louis and Billy when they came down. They send you their love. Louis writes to Jessie, but poor Billy doesn't write. He's good at making grenades from old jam tins. He sits for hours on the firestep hunched over his work like a gopher in its tunnel. That's what *trenches are like – gopher tunnels.*

   I have learned some new songs in the trench-
es. Here is one I will teach you when I get home.

There's a little wet home in the trench
that the rainstorms continually drench
A dead cow close by, with her hooves in the sky
And she gives off a terrible stench.
Underneath us in place of a floor
is a mess of cold mud and some straw,
And the Jack Johnsons roar
as they speed through the air
O'er my little wet home in the trench.

   I receive the papers right along and enjoy them
very much. I got the last one two days ago. I also
got mother's parcel o.k. with the cake, tobacco,
towels and handkerchiefs, everything was fine. I
think you make very nice fudge if I remember right,
don't you, of course I don't want you to go to the
trouble of making any to see if you could, but it
just struck me that you do. I will write to dear
Auntie Fannie who knitted me a balaclava. Well
everything comes to an end so here goes.

                              With love to all,
                                 Arnold

CHAPTER 35

April 3, 1917

There had been 200,000 British and French casualties in earlier attempts on Vimy Ridge. General Arthur Currie prepared meticulously when the Canadian Corps was given the assignment of taking Vimy Ridge. He believed that his attack troops should be "rested, fed, happy," and that other troops should do the dirty work for them.

Arnold, Louis and Billy were assigned to Signals, Arnold because he registered as a mechanic. He insisted that Louis and Billy were mechanics too, and that they must stay together. They did, but once the officers had sized the men up, only Arnold and Louis were kept as Signallers. They were all given rifles and expected to fight in the second and third waves as well as to do repairs to communications. Billy was kept in their unit. Not only was he a good shot with a rifle, but he was good at making grenades out of jam pot tins, which he did to keep busy. He lined the empty jam pots with burlap and mud, put in old nails and parts of shells, a primer of gun cotton, a copper detonator, and a fuse. When night raids were ordered on German trenches, Billy would crawl out ahead of the attack party, hide in a shell hole close to the German lines, light one of his grenades from a match, then throw it. The Canadians felt the raids a waste of life, but Billy enjoyed the adventure. He was good at it, and he was allowed to run back after he had thrown his grenade.

One hot April day at Vimy the three men were in a forward trench, dry, well-drained, formerly occupied by the French. Arnold and Louis had been sent out twice to repair a telephone wire to the forward observation post that was in the non-stop Canadian Artillery line of fire. The signal cables had been buried, but when some shells fell short of the German line, the cables were churned up and broken. When the order came to repair the line again, Arnold was in the latrine with dysentry. When he swayed out and got the order, he cursed.

"Tell them to hold off the goddamned artillery fire while we do it," he shouted, but the sergeant was well in the communication trench towards the back of the line.

"I'll go this time," Billy said, putting aside the makings of a grenade. "Me and Louis can do it. Louis knows how to do it, don't you, Louis?"

Louis looked pale. He had been covering his ears against the deafening Canadian artillery barrage. He didn't want to risk his life again for something that was constantly under fire, but he didn't want to be court-martialled for not obeying an order.

"Sure," he said weakly. "Come on, Billy." He climbed the ladder and began crawling into no-man's-land as he and Arnold had already done twice that day, checking the telephone line. Billy followed him. They had to crouch to do the repair. It was then the shell hit Billy, a direct hit. His body fell against Louis, splattering him. Louis clutched

Billy to him and staggered back to the trench. When Arnold saw Louis, weeping, with what was left of Billy plastered against him, he burst into tears, then scrambled out of the trench and guided Louis down the ladder.

When they wove their way back to the medical dugout, Charles looked up and took in the horror. He finished assisting a German doctor, a prisoner, in removing shrapnel from a patient, then moved, crying, to Arnold and Louis. Arnold did not recognized Charles – his hair had turned white – until he watched him tenderly clean Billy's body off Louis. He lifted an eye, one of those beautiful chickory flower eyes that Agnes had admired, off Louis's tunic, a bizarre military decoration. Charles and Arnold both had the impulse to keep the eye, it was such a work of art, but Charles placed it for burial with the rest of Billy's body.

Louis, in shock, weeping, reverted to speaking only French. Charles persuaded the doctor in charge to send him to a French hospital. That would get him out of the front line for a while.

Charles turned to Arnold and cleaned him up, replacing his soiled uniform with flannel pjamas. He had a high fever, trench fever caught from the fleas in the trenches. He was sent back to base camp to recover.

"Be ruthless in surviving, Buster," Charles said to him in a low voice when he led him out of the medical dugout. "Keep your head down always, don't dally at trench intersections or cross roads, never take the same route twice, hit the ground when bullets are flying and never volunteer. Survive, Buster." Charles gave him a little push in the right direction.

That night at 2929, Billy's dog howled non-stop. Agnes got out of bed and padded down to the basement in her slippers and robe to see what was wrong. There was nothing, but Roger whimpered on. She patted him, covered him with his blanket, but as soon as she was up the stairs, he howled again. "Here, we mustn't have that. You'll be keeping all the neighbours awake with that noise." Agnes untied him, tucked his blanket under one arm, and led him up to her bedroom. She made a bed for him on the floor. But as soon as she was tucked into bed, she felt Roger slide onto the bed beside her. *Well, there are worse things than sleeping with a dog,* she decided.

When the Ministry telegram came to 2929, addressed to Agnes, she could not stop shaking. It was her Arnold, her only living son, now sacrificed to what? There were embers in the fireplace. She raked them, then sat shaking until Jessie came in from work.

When Jessie saw the unopened telegram in her mother's hand, she went into the kitchen and made tea. She brought a tea tray and sat it next to Agnes, pouring her a cup, but Agnes seemed numb. Jessie poured herself a cup of tea and sat with her mother until Miriam came home. When Miriam sized up the situation, she got brandy from the medicine chest and forced a shot into her mother. Miriam took the telegram, opened it, and read it, looking puzzled.

"Oh, it's our Billy," she said. "We've lost our Billy."

Agnes stared at her and took the telegram. After she had read and reread it, she said, "His dog tried to tell me last night, but I was too thick to understand."

"Did you know he called himself Jackson and gave you as his next-of-kin?" Miriam asked.

Agnes shook her head. "It makes sense when you think of it," she said. "Who else could he give?"

That year Agnes wrote her first letter to the newspapers.

> *Dear Editor,*
>
> *Last week I received a telegram from the Department of Militia and Defence announcing that my son, William Jackson, was killed in action.*
>
> *This week I received a statement from His Majesty's government deducting from my son's pay account, which stopped the day he was killed, the price of the blanket my son was buried in. Is this what our sons are fighting and dying for?*

Agnes received another letter from the department refunding the price of the blanket and announcing a change in the policy.

CHAPTER 36

Summer, 1917

A rnold began to write to his mother, which he had not done since he went overseas, not even to acknowledge her parcels.

Dear Mother,

By now you will have had the bad news about Billy. I want you to know he died instantly, felt no pain, and Louis and I were with him. He was a great member of our family, and I will miss him keenly. Such a sport.

I am now in my fourth hospital, a base hospital, hoping to be transferred to Blighty for a rest, but few get that move. The pains have almost gone, but my temperature is varied and I feel weak. We are in large tents, 40 beds to a tent, and I can tell you it is mighty cold some days. We have had a hard frost the last few days but seems to have changed today for it is much warmer in bed. Anyway, a pair of white sheets and lots of blankets and a nice spring bed have got the old dugout and trenches beat a thousand different ways.

I should have written sooner only I didn't know I was going to be sick. I just blacked out, and Charles was on duty in our unit, so he got me out, and sent Louis, who must also have this trench fever, to a French hospital so he can talk French to some pretty French nurses. Well, I can't complain.

I sent a message to our unit at the front to send my mail here. I look for it every time they bring the mail. I tell you, what I do miss is reading. I did get about four bundles of magazines, thank you, but left them there. I had pictures taken and they are here in my haversack. You will notice I have lost quite a lot of weight since I was home. They may send me up the coast for convalescence.

Do you realize the letter in the last parcel you sent was addressed to Mrs. Mitchell? Is she at the front? At any rate, tell her I enjoyed all the treats you sent, and I hope she enjoys my cigarettes.

Tell the girls I will answer their letters and Auntie Fannie's as soon as I am fit. I am always looking for your letters and parcels.

Your son,
Arnold

CHAPTER 37

November 20, 1918, North Battleford Provincial Hospital

> Dear Mrs. Jackson,
>
> Your visit to the hospital in 1915 – what a long time ago – was most helpful both to me and to Mr. Jackson. When he saw you leave across the yard, he burst into tears, cried for many hours, and for a number of times since when I saw him he has cried. I know this must sound upsetting to you, but therapeutically nothing could help Mr. Jackson more. I have been able to suggest to him the great losses in his life, when he felt abandoned, and he has grieved appropriately. He now will talk to the staff, although he has little in common with our other patients. He doesn't belong here, as I said to you in 1915.
>
> Now that civilian train travel has been resumed, if you could guarantee a tranquil life, I will recommend that he be released into your care.
>
> I look forward to hearing from you.
>
> > Yours truly,
> > Anton Gaspard, M.D.

CHAPTER 38

Spring, 1919

Arnold was sent home to Earl Grey School, which had become a military hospital. He had a recurrence of the dysentry from trench fever, and Bright's disease. Agnes visited him daily, taking him nourishing foods, for he was very thin and withdrawn. Agnes also brought him family news, magazines and newspapers, but when she tried to get him to talk, he turned to the wall. She did not guess that he was wondering – *What can I possibly share with my mother or with Miriam of the last three years of my life, the slaughter?* He was afraid the fearful things would spill out of him to his mother, as they had when he was a child, but the three years took over his sleep, and he often woke sweating, with the dark brown smell of death around him.

When the Spanish Flu hit the hospital Arnold caught it. The doctor in charge asked Agnes to take Arnold home, his medical staff were dropping like flies. Agnes asked the doctor's back what she should do for Arnold. The doctor turned and said, "Get fluids into him now. Get him out of the house as soon as he's better. He's in danger of a major depression. The flu won't help that."

Agnes took Arnold home to his own room, and cooled his feverish body with wet flannels. When his fever broke, she fed him egg nogs and broth made from shin of beef. When he could sit up, Agnes went down with the flu, and Miriam and Jessie nursed them both. When it looked as if Agnes would not survive, Jessie broke down and cried in the living room. She and Miriam were sitting in their parents' chairs. Miriam went to her, sat on the arm of the chair, and tried to comfort Jessie, but she had little strength herself.

"I love her so, and I've never told her that," Jessie cried. "I've just grumbled, and she has been such a good mother to us."

Miriam cried too. "Well, we must do our best to keep her alive."

"I'm going to give up my job and stay home and look after them both," Jessie said.

Miriam did the arithmetic in her head. Yes, they could pay the bills on her wages, and Arnold was not yet discharged, so he and Agnes should be getting their army pay still. She patted Jessie's shoulder as consent.

With Jessie's devoted care, both patients recovered. Agnes's eyes had gummed together each time she awoke, which made Agnes feel blind, helpless. She would ring the little bell on her bedside table and Jessie would come in and sponge her mother's eyes open with a solution of boracic acid in warm water. When Agnes came downstairs to sit in the living room a little longer each day, Roger followed her. Miriam had allowed Roger to sleep in Agnes's room, but not on her bed. He sat on Agnes's feet when she sat in the living room.

"Take him up to Arnold," Agnes said. "See if Roger can get him out of bed. Say he needs to go for a walk."

But Roger could not get Arnold out of his room. No one could.

Jessie had begun reading the newspapers to Agnes, as she did when a child. She missed the fact that Canada had become a nation, a signator at the treaty of Versailles; that the Canadian troops had become the elite troops among the Allies, at a cost of 60,000 men to a country of eight million. Jessie noticed, "Oh, here's your friend Mrs. Pankhurst going to lecture at the City Hall auditorium. I didn't know she was in Canada."

"Let me see that," Agnes said, putting on her reading glasses. In two weeks Emmeline Pankhurst would be lecturing in Regina. Agnes would go and confront her about the feathers. Also tell her Canadian women had got the vote without slapping policemen, breaking windows and setting fires to post boxes.

Miriam thought it was too soon, too much for her mother to go out at night, but Agnes was adamant, and was soon back in her kitchen. Moreover she searched in the basement and found a white feather which she would give to Mrs. Emmeline Pankhurst. Miriam bought tickets for her mother and herself and ordered a taxi. Her own car was still under covers in the hardware storage building.

"She hasn't changed," Agnes said when she saw Mrs. Pankhurst up on the stage. But she had. She was older, frailer. Agnes gasped when Mrs. Pankhurst was introduced as sponsored by the National Council for Combatting Venereal Disease. Her talk was on moral hygiene, the evils of venereal disease, her audience mostly women. As Agnes sat through this "man-bashing" as she called it, she realized that Mrs. Pankhurst was still a woman of little means, and what she could do to earn money was to attract audiences and to lecture on whatever she would be paid for. *She's having to sell herself like a prostitute,* Agnes decided. When Mrs. Pankhurst referred to venereal disease among the veterans as a self-inflicted wound, Agnes stood and leaned towards Miriam. "I'm going home," she said. She and Miriam walked out before the lecture was over. Getting into the taxi, Agnes dropped the white feather into the gutter.

CHAPTER 39

March 8, 1919, North Battleford Provincial Hospital

Dear Mrs. Jackson,

I look forward to hearing from you, as your husband is ready for discharge. My staff have been devastated by the Spanish Flu. We are very short of help. The patients so far have not been affected.

If finances are a factor, I wonder if you know that Mr. Jackson has been receiving a small remittance from his family in England, which we have been banking for him. He could pay for his keep in a modest way.

Yours sincerely,
Anton Gaspard, M.D.

CHAPTER 40

Spring, 1919

Charles wrote from Kingston, Ontario, where he was reunited with his family. He had got a job as chief accountant with the Soldiers' Settlement Board in Regina. He was reluctant to travel with Deborah and Lawrence because of the prevalence of the Spanish Flu, but Deborah was actively miserable in Kingston. She wanted to share with her family Lawrence's daily changes in development.

Deborah wrote to say she so missed Christmas, 1918, with her family that she was not going to miss Easter. The Wilson family did not celebrate the way her family did.

"Regardless of the risks to the baby," Agnes said to Jessie. "Write and tell her no one celebrated Christmas last year. We were all too sick, too heart-sick."

"No, our Mum, they are coming anyway. Let's just make them feel welcome," Jessie said. She moved herself back into Miriam's room.

When the young family arrived wearing gauze masks, Deborah handed her toddler to Jessie, and examined the house from the outside. "Those storm windows should be down by now, Mother," she announced.

Agnes bit her tongue. With the house in quarantine and only women except for Arnold, who did she have to take off the storm windows and put on screens?

Charles was dismayed that Arnold would not come out of his room, nor receive Charles in it. Arnold could be heard having a bath or shaving in the middle of the night, but during the day he lived like a ghost upstairs, seeing only Jessie or Miriam who brought him food and newspapers and books, and changed his linen.

Charles was fulfilled in his new job caring for the veterans, but at home he missed the company of men. Deborah needed to involve him, when he got home from work, in every domestic detail of her day. He could not get past her to talk to Agnes or Miriam. They assumed it was courteous to allow the young family time to themselves, which was what Deborah wanted, but Charles longed for different voices.

One evening he came downstairs after Deborah was asleep. Agnes was sitting by the embers reading *Middlemarch*, her dog on her feet. She liked escaping in books into other people's lives.

"Would you mind if I joined you? I'm having trouble sleeping," Charles asked. He prodded the embers and added a piece of coal.

"Please join me," Agnes said. "I miss our chats from before the war."

"First I want to know how Mr. Jackson is. I miss him."

"I miss him too...I went to see him during the war...I forget when it was...and met his doctor, who writes me. Apparently my visit helped my husband...but I haven't been able to go back...I've been sick...and...." She didn't want to tell anyone that the doctor said that when he saw

Agnes leave the hospital, Edward burst into uncontrollable sobbing. But Agnes could not go back to North Battleford and leave her husband crying there. It haunted her. The doctor wanted her to bring him home, but she had been too sick, and now she had a houseful to feed.

"So you like George Eliot?" Charles asked.

But Agnes had other concerns. "Charles," she said, "I know about Billy. But what about Louis? I have to know."

Charles covered his mouth with his hands, his forehead furrowed. Then resting his hands on his knees he leaned forward saying, "Mrs. Jackson, I just don't know. I had him sent to a French hospital when he...was injured and Billy.... His mother was Belgian, you know, and he spoke French.... But then, he just disappeared. He's listed as missing, presumed dead. It wasn't a bad injury he had. I can't understand it. I've put in so many enquiries about him.... What about Jessie, Mrs. Jackson? Deborah tells me Louis was engaged to her."

"Engaged? Well, hardly. There were a few letters back and forth, but Jessie's heart seems elsewhere. She gets daily letters from a veteran teaching up north of Maidstone."

Agnes thought back to last summer when Miriam and Jessie had headed off in Miriam's car towards Regina Beach. They had been rolling down the Lumsden hill when they had a flat tire. That was one reason Agnes did not approve of Miriam driving a car – flat tires. The other was running out of gas. But they were saved by a provincial police sergeant, Tom Richards, whom Miriam had met before, and his friend Leon Van Gorder, on leave from the army. After the men had changed the tire, they put the car in reverse, pushed it up the hill, and persuaded the girls to return to Regina. They were invited in to dinner. Tom Richards recognized Agnes and the house. Leon Van Gorder recognized Jessie's beauty.

Agnes wondered what to tell Jessie. She had seemed pleased to have an embarkation present from Louis and the odd letter, but she seemed not too important to him, nor he to her. But it was hard to tell with her girls. They didn't confide in her much, perhaps because she had never confided in them.

CHAPTER 41

June, 1919, 2929 12th Avenue, Regina, Sask.

Dear Dr. Gaspard,

I am sorry to be long in answering your letters, but our house has been in quarantine for the Spanish Flu. My son, who was invalided home with Bright's Disease, caught the Flu in hospital and then I came down with it, and have but recently recovered. My married daughter, her husband, and child have just moved in with me. My son does not leave his room. So I cannot guarantee a tranquil life, much as I would like to have my husband home.

Yours sincerely,
Agnes Jackson

CHAPTER 42

Summer, 1919

An ebullient letter came to Agnes from Louis in Wales. He was fine, married to the French nurse who had saved his life, and was on his way home to find a job that would make him rich. His wife assumed he was a rich Canadian. He sent a picture of them both. Germaine was a head taller than Louis, slim, and of dark complexion like Miriam. Could Agnes put him up until he found a job?

Agnes shared the letter with the family at the dinner table. Where could they put Louis? In the box room, Jessie decided. So much for Louis's constancy.

Driving Louis home from the station, Miriam told him not to expect to see Arnold, that he had become a recluse. Louis would not accept that. He had become heavier, and had deep pockets under his eyes. His first dinner was a celebration. Agnes had killed and roasted two of her chickens. Deborah complained to the men of how the civilians had suffered during the war with rationing, meatless Fridays, and lineups for food. Charles interrupted her complaints to ask Louis about France, but Deborah chided him for interrupting her. With Deborah a married woman, Agnes felt less able to put a stop to her chatter.

When Jessie took his dinner up to Arnold, Louis went to the foot of the staircase, did a soft-shoe dance and called up, "What kind of chicken do you call this, Mrs. Jackson? There's no shot in it. I can't eat chicken without shot!"

After dinner Louis sat at the piano and began playing and singing *"Roses are Blooming in Picardy."* Charles, alarmed, came and stood at the piano and shook his head. Louis switched to playing chords. "No music?" he mouthed to Charles.

"Not that one," Charles said quietly. Louis tried *"Mademoiselle from Armentieres"* and Charles nodded. Jessie sang with him as she cleared the table. Deborah had evolved into a matron. She no longer sang, nor did she help with the housework. She went upstairs to check on her Lawrence. Agnes and Miriam were in the kitchen, washing up. Charles went back to reading the newspapers.

Louis strummed the piano, then sang:

When this bloody war is over
Oh how happy I will be
No more pork and beans for breakfast
No more bully beef for tea
When I get my civvy clothes on
No more soldiering for me

No one seemed to like that one. Louis sat at the piano, lost in thought. Then he sang, as if singing up the stairs to Arnold:

Nobody knows how tired we are
tired we are, tired we are

Nobody knows how tired we are
and nobody seems to care

Louis played chords again until he found another one he wanted, and sang softly, hoping the words would not reach the kitchen:

Do your balls hang low?
Do they dangle to and fro?
Can you tie them in a knot?
Can you tie them in a bow?

Charles had developed a short fuse overseas. He slapped his newspaper down and stood. Louis was irrepressible. He sang on:

Do you get them in a tangle?
Do you catch them in the mangle?
Do they swing in stormy weather?
Do they tickle with a feather?

Agnes was at the kitchen door, outraged, Miriam and Jessie looking over her shoulders. She would put a stop to this. What had happened to Louis that he would dare to sing bar room songs in her house? Then she heard, they all heard, careful steps coming down the stairs. Arnold stood in the hall in his felt slippers and bathrobe, looking at Louis. His brown hair had receded. His hands and feet were swollen. He walked stiffly. Louis couldn't resist the last verse:

Do they rattle when you walk?
Do they jingle when you talk?
Can you sling them on your shoulder?

Like a lousy fucking soldier?
Do your balls hang low?

Arnold gave a little chuckle. Louis got up and embraced him. They clung together, Charles standing by, waiting to be included.

"I thought your number was up," Arnold said, his voice phlegmy with disuse.

"I had a miraculous escape," Louis said, including Charles in the hug. "Look at this man. The Boche plucked his head like a chicken."

"My Charles is not a plucked chicken," Deborah cried running down the stairs.

Arnold looked at Charles and shook his hand. Charles had gone not only grey, but also bald. The three stood, hugging each other.

Agnes took Deborah and Jessie by the arm and led them into the kitchen. "Let the men have some time to themselves," she said, closing the kitchen door.

CHAPTER 43

Summer, 1919

Louis produced a bottle of Scotch he had brought from Wales against Canada's new prohibition law. Charles did not refuse. Overseas he found his tot of rum not only warming, but a way of relating to the other men. Here he would drink on principle because it was prohibited. He raised his glass and said, "Well, we three have endured the unendurable. We're together again."

"To absent friends," Louis said. They turned to the firestool where Billy used to sit and lifted their glasses to it.

When they sat, Charles noticed the label *Haig* on the bottle. He stood and threw the rest of his drink in the fire. Louis protested.

"I will not drink that butcher's whiskey," he said. "That wicked, evil man comes from this rich, whiskey-producing family." He brandished the bottle. Louis looked fearful that he would smash it.

"I read up on him in Kingston," Charles went on. "He failed from Oxford into Sandhurst, bought a commission with this whiskey money, and sent men by the hundreds of thousands into certain death in swampy open fields. If I ever get a chance, I will shoot that bastard. And any of the politicians who were playing power games with our lives."

The other two laughed.

"This is Charles, who wouldn't shoot a prairie chicken?" Arnold said.

"Speaking of which, shall we go out tomorrow morning, Buster?" Louis asked. "The little bleeders must have generations of progeny waiting for us."

Arnold shook his head and sipped his Scotch. "I've done enough killing to last my lifetime. I don't want to have a gun in my hand ever again...I'll give it to Charles. Well, you two, you're both married men. What's it like?"

Charles's forehead furrowed. "It's hard to say. I didn't know what to expect, so I'm continually being surprised at what is expected of me. I always thought that marriage would be based on understanding – that it wouldn't have to be verbalized because you understood each other – that it would be being together but not necessarily interacting all the time. I imagine women take to marriage more than men do. They like to talk, don't they?"

Arnold and Louis smiled and stayed silent. They both wanted to say that Charles too liked to talk, but Deborah did so in a flood of words, without topic sentences or paragraphs or awareness of her listeners so that others had to filter for meaning. In the silence Charles stared at the fire, realizing he would have to live with what he had settled into by a hasty, needy decision. Yet he was no longer lonely or needy. Perhaps this was what life offered, and one adjusted to the intolerable in another in exchange for acceptance of one's own intolerable habits. Which were his?

"What about you, Louis? What is Germaine like?" Arnold asked.

Louis laughed. "I'm not sure. I feel I hardly know her.

She was nursing me, you know, in Paris. Then when the army made enquiries about me being ready to go back to the front, she and the nuns told them I had been moved to convalescence in a non-existent village. Germaine hid me with her family. I knew I would be slaughtered if I went back and so did they. So somehow we were married, and she is going to have our child, and I, being a rich Canadian, have come home to make my fortune." Louis smiled at his irony. "From what I see, Canada seems to have done well out of the war."

"Not the veterans and their families," Charles said grimly. "But that's going to change."

"Charles, why did you stop me playing *"Roses in Picardy"*?" Louis asked.

Charles took a deep breath and reached into a part of himself he had not shared with anyone. He chose his words with care. "Because Jack Foxxe was killed at the Somme, which is in Picardy."

"You were at the Somme?" Arnold asked, incredulous.

"For two long months," Charles said.

"No wonder you lost your hair," Louis said.

Arnold got up and leaned against the mantelpiece, staring at the fire. He had not answered Jack's letters to him.

"I had forgotten to ask about Jack," Louis said. "I suppose being one of the first to go, you wouldn't expect him to survive. Wasn't I lucky they wouldn't accept me in 1915?"

But Charles and Arnold did not want to dismiss Jack so quickly. Arnold turned, went to the bottle and poured a drink in three glasses.

"I suppose that being an officer, he didn't feel like one of us," Louis said.

Charles could not refuse."To Jack," they said, standing,

raising their glasses and drinking.

"How is Miriam taking it?" Charles asked Arnold.

"Stoically," Arnold said. "Mother guesses that she knew long before it happened. Apparently the daily casualty lists in the newspapers were horrendous. We were spared that, knowing only what we saw, and that was bad enough. But she's bright, and she would know his name would appear. Mother guesses that the Jack part of her died before he did...Mother keeps in touch with his parents, but Miriam can't bear to see them often."

"Are they still down in Lakeview?"

Arnold realized that he had taken in all the gossip when his sisters were bringing him food. They had talked into his vacuum, hoping to bring him back, he supposed. And they did. "No. Apparently the old man broke up when he heard about Jack. They've come down in the world – moved out on the prairie on Horace Street where he can have a large garden. But what he does in the long winters away out there, I can't guess. Well, yes, I can. They took in our Julia, the cleaning lady, when she produced a child. And the old man looks after him while the women work...what did the girls tell me about the mother? That she opened a shop."

"And sells gowns," Louis guessed.

"No, second-hand furniture, actually. She couldn't get a good price when they had to sell their big house, so she opened a shop on Hamilton Street across from *The Leader.* And is doing quite well apparently. She buys up furniture of people moving to the Coast and sells it to...whoever. The women are different now. They got the vote, you know, while we were overseas. Without fighting for it as my mother had to do."

Arnold listened to himself talk. How many months, was it years, since he had talked?

Charles thought of Deborah as a woman with a vote. He wondered if he could persuade her to vote with him, or would she vote with the Conservatism that characterized this family?

They sat in silence staring at the fire.

Then Louis asked, "Charles, know of any jobs that pay better than sales?"

"I might," Charles said. "My job is to help veterans settle back into civilian life."

"Is that what you are going to do for the rest of your life?"

"Oh no. I've begun taking chartered accountancy at night school." Charles stood and paced, speaking with passion. "When I qualify, I will never again work for another man. I will never again salute another man, or bow or kneel to him. We three should not give our power, our lives, over into the hands of other men. We should make a society of equals. Here in Canada." He stopped and looked at the other two. "Help me! The three of us could work together, preferably for ourselves, or in co-operation with like-minded men and have nothing to do with men who exploit or make use of others."

Arnold heard his mother in his head, *He is a fool that cannot conceal his wisdom.*

"You sound like a politician," Louis said. "Thinking of going into politics, Charles?"

Charles gave a little smile of pleasure. "I might. If an Oppositionist party forms. The important thing in a democracy is accountability. We now know that people in responsible positions will not behave responsibly unless we make them. Yes, Canada has the problem of throwing off colonialism, stopping being butchered by Europeans in the name of kings and emperors. We must refuse to fight their games for them. Help me."

Arnold rummaged in his bathrobe pockets for cigarettes, offered one to Louis, and lit it for him. He was not interested in politics. "It's all very well for you, Charles. You have a trade that people want. Louis and I are relatively unskilled."

Is Arnold driven to sink his own ship? Charles wondered. *What's happened to his independence?*

"Arnold, what do you want to do with the rest of your life?"

"Certainly not get married, listening to you two," he chuckled. Then he stared at the fire. "When I was convalescing, I was reading Kierkegaard. He said that whatever choices you make, like marrying or not marrying, you will have regrets, but in the end man chooses himself. I think I have reached that end, after what we've been through. What I like doing most is building houses, but I haven't the capital to start. I would have to have a job and save. I have my mother to support, you know."

"Louis?"

"We all have women to support, and children too. Feeding and housing them comes before dreams."

Charles jumped in. "But we only live once, and we must make our dreams happen. Otherwise we will be living lives dictated by other people. Look, we veterans have demanded the government give us $2,000 compensation for income we lost in the war, and loans to help us get a start in business, or to build ourselves houses. We can start a building society, why not a people's bank, and use their money to build houses for them. What people will always need is food and shelter. The rest changes."

"You want to be in the building trade?" Arnold asked, skeptical.

"Not in the actual construction, no, but the business end, yes. We could do it on the side at first, one house at a time."

"Mine," joked Louis.

Charles looked dismayed. With one child and another on the way, he needed a house sooner than Louis.

"Louis?" Arnold asked. "You interested in building?"

Louis laughed and looked at the ceiling. "Buster, you know how good I'd be with a hammer and nails. You'd be cursing me all the time. No, I like sales because I like people. I'm wondering about trying to get a second job at night in hotels singing and playing the piano."

Charles and Arnold stared at the fire, subdued. Arnold thought of Billy and how handy he would be at building. He rubbed his fists into his eyes the way Billy had done in the trenches. He wondered if Billy had had double vision, the side effect of Arnold's nephritis, or was it exhaustion. Would Billy have been helped by spectacles? Arnold should have thought of that while he was alive.

"You could be our salesperson," Charles said.

"For one house a year?"

"Well, we have to start somewhere. Arnold..."

"Call me Buster," Arnold said.

"Your mother doesn't."

"She's the only one."

"Okay, Buster, I have some money saved up – enough to buy a lot. Why don't we go out and look at lots in this neighbourhood tomorrow."

"In this neighbourhood?"

"Why not? Deborah wants to live around the corner from her mother and sisters."

CHAPTER 44

Summer, 1919

When Arnold had been back at work at the hardware store for a week, Agnes sat next to him on the porch on a warm Sunday afternoon. She had two folded letters in her hand. Arnold put down his newspaper, sensing she wanted to talk.

"Now that you're better, I have to deal with these letters from North Battleford about your father," she said.

Arnold took the letters to please his mother, but he didn't read them. He put them in his pocket.

"He's not coming back here," he announced. A cold fury towards his father had sat like a hailstone inside him since he was a child. During the war it had grown to an iceberg.

"He has to. He has nowhere else to go."

"He's not coming here," Arnold said, taking off his new reading glasses and closing his eyes.

"Oh, Arnold, why are you so Old Testament, so short on forgiveness and compassion? We can't leave him in that institution. He would rot there."

"Not my problem."

"He is your problem. We're his next of kin."

"You may be, but I'm not. He didn't provide for me when I was a kid. He hit me."

Agnes bit her lip and stood up. "This is no way to live, licking your childhood wounds, being so hard on others," she said.

That evening was a dinner celebration of Jessie's engagement to Leon Van Gorder. Agnes cooked a prime rib roast, Yorkshire pudding, and roasted potatoes. She had iced a sponge cake with lemon icing and lit nineteen candles on it, even though it wasn't exactly a birthday. Van's friend Tom Richards sat next to Miriam. He had lost his wife to tuberculosis; she had lost her Jack.

To fit in the guests, Arnold ended up sitting in his father's old seat opposite his mother. If he noticed, he did not say, the conversation criss-crossing the table was so lively.

When his mother glanced at him, she wondered how he could sit there, with his quiet chuckle, more like a throaty bubbling after the war, as if they had not discussed her major problem – what to do about Edward – that very afternoon. Had he read the letters from Dr. Gaspard? No, not his problem, he'd said. Well, perhaps he had suffered enough during the war, and did not want to deal with his father's suffering.

After the young had played cards and sung around the piano, the guests had gone home and the others up to bed, Arnold sat in his father's chair in the living room for a last smoke. What was his mother thinking? What would she do? He leaned his head back and closed his eyes. When he did that, he began to sweat. His nostrils filled with the dark brown smell of death. He opened his eyes and leaned forward, staring at what was left of the fire. He couldn't think this way, leaning forward. He stood up and began pacing around the house, his house. In the dining room, he realized that the table, so full of life these days, would empty as Charles and Deborah, Louis, Jessie and her man would move out. And yes, Miriam would probably marry, she was so wonderful.

And that would leave...himself and his mother, and if she insisted, his father. He would come home to the silent meals of his past. He could not bear it. And if his father died first, he would still have his mother to support. He would become his father. He could not bear it.

Yet, if she were here, they would come back for all the celebrations that she planned and cooked for. He had no choice. Had he ever had a choice? Arnold sat at the empty dining table until dawn.

That night Agnes slept for the last time in that room, her arm around her dog. The next day while Julia and Jessie were doing the washing and cleaning, Agnes was travelling upstairs and downstairs packing a trunk and suitcase. By noon she was dressed in her Sunday best, her trunk packed, a half-packed suitcase for Edward.

Now Jessie," she said, "you just drive me to the station. I'm going to visit your father."

"But you don't need all this luggage, our mum, just for a visit. Where will you stay?"

"I don't know, but I'll write you. Now, let's be off."

Sitting beside Jessie in Miriam's Model T, Agnes gave one glance to 2929, then looked straight ahead.

ACKNOWLEDGMENTS:

To my Cousins: This is a work of imagination drawn from the lives of Grannie and our parents. You will have other impressions. I look forward to reading them.

Thanks to my colleagues in the West End Writers' Club for their insights.

Thanks to my sister, Ruth Charnell, and cousin Ed Parkin, for driving with me to Regina.

Thanks to my mentor, George McWhirter, and to my editor, Geoffrey Ursell. Thanks also to Ken Aitken of the Regina Public Library Prairie History Room, where I spent many happy hours reading:

Earl G. Drake, *Regina the Queen City*, Montreal, McLelland & Stewart, 1955

J. W. Brennan, co-ordinator, *Regina before yesterday, a visual history, 1889-1995*, Saskatchewan Archives Board

J. W. Brennan, *Regina, an illustrated history*, Toronto, James Lorimer, 1989

W. A. Riddell, *Regina from Pile of Bones to Queen City*, Burlington Ontario, Windsor Publications, 1981

Frank Anderson, *Regina's Terrible Tornado*, Calgary, Frontier Publications, 1964, 1968

Gein, Stuart A.G., *Up the Johns! the Story of the Royal Regina Rifles*, North Battleford, Senate of RRR, 1992

Prairie History Room, Regina Public Library, file on the Regina Tornado, 1912

Regina Board of Trade, *Regina, the Capital of Saskatchewan, 1906*

J.S. Woodsworth, *Report of a Preliminary and General Social Survey of Regina*, Dept. of Temperance and Moral Reform of the Methodist Church and the Board of Social Service & Evangelism of the Presbyterian Church, September, 1913

Gordon Howard, *60 years of Centennial in Saskatchewan*, typed copy, no date, 146pp

Copies of *The Leader* newpapers, 1910 – 1920

Marguerite E. Robinson, *History of Wascana Creek*, Sask. Dept. of Culture & Youth, Local Histories Program, 1976

P. McAra, *62 Years on the Saskatchewan Prairies*, 1945

Thanks to the librarians at the Manchester Public Library for:

Hannah Mitchell, *The Hard Way up*, London, Faber & Faber, 1967

Barbara Castle, *Sylvia & Christabel Pankhurst*, London, Penguin, 1987

Jon Glover & Jon Silkin, *First World War Prose*, London, Viking, 1989

Dennis Winter, *Haig's Command*, London, Viking, 1991

Lyn MacDonald, *1915 the Death of Innocence*, London, Hodder Headline, 1993

Rev. William Barker, *The Mother Church of Manchester, Primitive Methodism*, Manchester & London, Percy Brothers, 1928

Michael Sheard, *Primitive Methodism in Manchester Area*, Wesley Historical Society, Lancashire & Cheshire, occasional publication #4, 1976

G.E. Milburn, *A School for the Prophets, the Origins of Ministerial Education in Primitive Methodist Church*, Manchester, Hartley Victoria College

Methodism in Moss Side for 90 Years, Great Western Street Methodist Church, 1968

Thanks to the Vancouver Public Library for:

Desmond Morton, *When Your Number's Up: The Canadian Soldier in the First World War*, Toronto, Random House of Canada, 1993

Desmond Morton, *Marching to Armageddon: Canadians and the Great War*, Toronto, Lester, Orpen Dennys, 1989

D.J. Goodspeed, *The Road Past Vimy: The Canadian Corps, 1914-1918*, Toronto, Macmillan of Canada, 1969

Vera Brittain, *Testament of Youth*, New York, Macmillan, 1933

Sandra Gwyn, *Tapestry of War*, Toronto, Harper Collins, 1992

Lyn Bowen, *Muddling Through: the Remarkable Story of the Barr Colonists*, Vancouver, Douglas & McIntyre, 1992

George Woodcock, *The Canadians*, Don Mills, Fitzhenry & Whiteside, 1979

Edward McCourt, *Saskatchewan*, Toronto, Macmillan, 1968

John H. Archer, *Saskatchewan, A History*, Saskatoon, Western Producer, 1980

Daphne Read, *The Great War and Canadian Society*, Toronto, Hogton Press, 1978

JULIA VAN GORDER is a distinctive new voice in Canadian Fiction. She has published fiction, poetry and non-fiction nationally and internationally, in such publications as *CVII*, *Descant*, *Event*, *Poetry Nottingham International*, *Prairie Fire*, *Prism*, *Redoubt*, *Room of One's Own*, *Western People*, and *Treeline*, an Internet publication. Her fiction has also been featured on the BBC World Service.

A retired social worker and high school counsellor, Julia was born in Regina and raised on the Canadian prairies. She has lived in London and Oxford. She now lives in Vancouver.

Cyclone is her first published book.